PETER AND THE SERPENT

Ralph W Osgood II

TABLE OF CONTENTS

Magie Lantern
PRODUCTIONS

MEMO

from the desk of

Howard G Kazanjian

Sweeping action, adventure and great characters make great stories. Readers will be swept away with Ralph Osgood's Peter and the Serpent as the characters come alive.

With twist and turns Osgood's story of an orphan boy escaping his cruel master while risking everything including his life to find his father. With spiritual overtones this story captivates the reader.

When Ralph gets interested in a subject, nothing stops him until his idea is on paper. This story is unique because of the London location in the mid seventeen hundreds. It captures one's imagination.

Ralph Osgood is a movie buff as well as a movie history buff. This is a must read.

Howard G Kazanjian
    Exec. Producer - The Empire Strikes Back, Return of the Jedi, Raiders of the Lost Ark

DON'T MISS THESE BOOKS FROM MR KAZANJIAN

While still keeping his hand in the film business, Howard Kazanjian is hard at work as an author. With his writing partner, former stunt woman Chris Enns, he has written seven histories of the Old West, touching on such personages as Annie Oakley, Sam Sixkiller, Bat Masterson, Wyatt Earp, General Armstrong Custer and his bride Libby Custer, and others.

To date he has also contributed four film related books:
Happy Trails: a Celebration of the Life and Times of Roy Rogers and Dale Evans
The Young Duke: The Early Life of John Wayne
The Cowboy and the Señorita: A Biography of Roy Rogers and Dale Evans
Cowboys, Creatures, and Classics: The Story of Republic Pictures
And the just released:
Straight Lady: The Life and Times of Margaret Dumont, "The Fifth Marx Brother"

And not to be missed is the biography about Howard by J. W. Rinzler:
Howard Kazanjian: A Producer's Life.
In which you can follow his career as a graduate from USC as he started in television with Four Star Productions, moving to Warner Brothers and feature films as an assistant director. In that capacity he worked with such directors as:
Bill Conrad
Sam Peckinpah
Josh Logan
Elia Kazan
Francis Ford Coppola
After a short sojourn at Disney in the 1970s he landed at Universal and worked with:
Billy Wilder
Robert Wise
Alfred Hitchcock
From there he moved over to Lucas Film with his fellow USC grad, George Lucas, and together made cinema history.

SOME NOTES TO MY READERS

I think that a few words about screenplay format might be instructive for those readers who may not be familiar with it. Just like a novel there are passages of description and action, with dialogue attached to the character who speaks.

What may be unfamiliar are the additional words and forms that box in the first two types of passages.

First one to explain is the slug line, all in capitals, it designates the beginning of a scene. The abbreviations are a shorthand for relaying to the reader the most fundamental elements of the scene - interior (INT) or exterior (EXT); followed by the name of the setting; followed by whether it transpires in the daytime (DAY) or nighttime (NIGHT).

Slugline example from this screenplay:

INT. GARRET ROOM - DAY (LONDON 1742)

At the beginning of a screenplay there may be (as in mine) an additional parenthetical statement that gives a broader idea of the setting and time period.

More slug lines can follow the initial one for a scene, as focus changes within the same scene onto a particular character, another part of the setting, or a different time within the set scene. You will know when a scene changes when the next INT or EXT appears.

INT/EXT or EXT/INT - denoting movement from one to the other.

Secondly, here are some abbreviations that are helpful to know:

O.S. - Off scene - whether it is the character or a sound you will know from its placement in the text.

O.C. - Off camera - present in the scene but not in view of the camera.

P.O.V. - Point of view - indicates that we are being shown what the character is seeing.

MOS - without sound.

V.O. - Voice over - the character is commenting about the scene you are watching. His memory of what transpired.

Remember a screenplay is a blueprint to be used in creating a captured performance on film. So I would encourage you that it is not that different from a novel where the world is formed inside your head as you read the words on the page. You can have the same experience reading a screenplay by allowing the writer to direct your inner eye to see his vision.

Although the script in this size paperback format weighs in at 176 pages, in the normal size paper format for film scripts it comes in at 115 pages.

OTHER IDEAS THAT MAY HELP YOU VISUALIZE THIS SCREENPLAY

Screenwriters often write with certain actors in mind. I had a few in mind as I wrote Peter and the Serpent.

Roger Morgan - Mel Gibson
   Jerry (the giant) - John Goodman
   Andrew Simms   - Jim Carrey
   Abram Dumbleton - Dean Jones

You may have a few of your own as you go through the script.

Go for it.

FADE IN:

INT. GARRET ROOM - DAY (LONDON 1742)

Three boys lie asleep in a straw bed.
A fourth, PETER MICKLEWHITE, awake,
sits gazing out the window. They are
chimney-sweeps, all begrimed and soot
smeared. GABRIEL, the boy next to
Peter mumbles.

> GABRIEL
> It's cold, Peter!

He pulls the blanket end from Peter
and wraps it around himself.

> PETER
> Sun'll be up soon.

Peter grabs the blanket end back and
tucks it around his legs. The links of
a chain RATTLE as he does so.

> PETER (CONT'D)
> Don't you want to see it?

For answer Gabriel rolls over away
from Peter. A RATTLE.

> PETER (CONT'D)
> You don't know what you're
> missing.

> GABRIEL
> Everyone's seen the sun.

Peter jumps out of bed and over to the

window. Gabriel waits a beat, then rolls out to join him. Rubbing his eyes, he hops up on the sill beside Peter.

THE BOYS' P.O.V.

The city of London stretches off to the sunrise. The spires of the city's many churches would be the tallest forms against the sky if it were not for the countless streaks of coal-fire smoke streaming to the heavens.

PETER AND GABRIEL

Gabriel, now awake, looks down at Peter's hands, busy sketching a man on a horse.

> GABRIEL
> Who's that?

> PETER
> My father.

> SECOND BOY
> Shut up! We're trying to sleep!

> THIRD BOY
> He doesn't have a father!

They roll over and bury their heads.

> GABRIEL
> (whispers)
> Show me the one of Mr. Black again.

Peter shakes his head. Gabriel pleads silently. Peter relents and takes out a folded scrap.

THE SKETCH OF MR. BLACK

a visage of malevolence - a giant head attached to a tiny body.

THE DOOR

Bursts open and the subject of the sketch enters the room.

> BLACK
> Everybody up! We gotta job.

His jaw drops when he sees two boys already are.

Peter and Gabriel, stupid with surprise, stand frozen by the window. Black grabs the piece of paper out of Gabriel's hands, looks at it and explodes. He rips it to pieces and tosses them and the pencil out the window.

> GABRIEL
> I dinna do it, Mr. Black! It were Peter!

Black collars Peter about the neck and marches him out of the room.

> BLACK
> You'll regret this. The rest of you - downstairs! Now!

LOWER ROOM

Feeney, a runt of a man waits by the front door.

                    FEENEY
          About time! The Bishop's not
          a man to be kept waiting!

                    BLACK
          Just a minute more, Mr.
          Feeney.

Black takes down a key, unlocks Peter's chains, then does the same for the other boys as they troop into the room. He hangs the shackles on the wall.

He clouts Peter behind his ear. Then flashes a smile at Feeney.

                    BLACK (CONT'D)
          Now, we're ready!

EXT. A FIELD - DAY

Feeney leads Black and his four sweeps across a field at the edge of London towards a mansion just visible over a rise.

INT. THE BISHOP'S PALACE/BISHOP'S CHAMBER - DAY

Ancient tomes line equally ancient bookshelves and clutter the desk before the BISHOP OF LONDON - EDMUND GIBSON.

            GIBSON
Your views are well known,
because you have made them
well known.

He holds aloft a pamphlet, then lets
it fall with a SMACK on the desk
before his visitor, GEORGE WHITEFIELD,
standing across the desk from him.

            GEORGE
There is nothing there which
is not true. Nowhere have I
deviated from the truth of
Scripture.

            GIBSON
Nowhere in Scripture are you
commanded to denigrate your
brothers in the ministry.
Rather, you are commanded
otherwise.

The thick oak door behind George opens
with a CREAK, and Feeney enters.

            FEENEY
Pardon, your Grace, but the
chimney sweeps are here.

            GIBSON
Well.. Did you expect to
start them here? Use some
common sense, man! Start
them in the room next door.

            FEENEY
Very good, your Grace.

He departs, closing the door with
care.

IN THE HALL

Feeney leads the sweeps to the next
room. Black looks inside.

> BLACK
> (to the two older boys)
> You two go with Mr. Feeney,
> he'll show you where to set
> the ladder. Then meet us
> back in here.

ROOM WITH A LARGE FIREPLACE

Black eyes Peter and motions with a
jerk of his head that he's to go up
the shaft. Peter looks at Gabriel,
then steps into the fireplace opening.

INSIDE THE CHIMNEY

Peter lifts his soot stained face to
the chimney opening, reaches forward
and finds a hand-hold. He pulls
himself up into the narrowing flue and
stops to catch his breath.

He overhears voices speaking below. He
halts to listen.

> GIBSON (O.S.)
> I have to say no. I cannot
> allow you the pulpits of
> this city.

THE BISHOP'S CHAMBER

                    GEORGE
          Will you allow me, at the
          least, to take up a
          collection for my orphanage?

                    GIBSON
          Ah, yes, the orphanage. You
          have, of course, already met
          with the Georgia Colony
          Trustees?

                    GEORGE
          Yes, your Grace. They have
          other financial concerns at
          present.

Gibson purses his lips in thought.

                    GIBSON
          If you are taking a
          subscription, you may put me
          down for 10 pounds. How much
          are you needing to raise?

                    GEORGE
          In total, we owe a thousand
          pounds.

IN THE HALL

A bent Feeney listens at the keyhole.

                    GIBSON (O.S.)
          A thousand pounds!!??

Another NOISE causes Feeney to
straighten and step away.

INSIDE THE CHIMNEY

As quietly as he can, Peter works with

his brushes.

                    GEORGE (O.S.)
          Aye, a princely sum, and the
          reward for presumption on my
          part. The promise of
          financial support from my
          friend and colleague William
          Seward, ended when he died
          intestate last year.

                    GIBSON (O.S.)
          Presumption, indeed, when
          death is not provided for.

                    GEORGE (O.S.)
          I am certain that the Lord
          will answer my prayers for
          my orphans.

ROOM WITH A LARGE FIREPLACE

Black paces back and forth in front of
the fireplace. Gabriel stands idle
with a broom and scuttle. When Feeney
enters Black stops in front of the
mantel, bends down, and looks up the
flue.

                    BLACK
          Damme! Petey, if you ain't
          down here in three ticks
          you'll have a hidin' instead
          o' your supper!

Peter sobs and says something but it
is muffled.

                    BLACK (CONT'D)
          What was that? I'll take no
                    (MORE)

>   BLACK (CONT'D)
> insolence from the likes of
> you.

INSIDE THE CHIMNEY

Peter descends, his body quaking. He
loses his grasp on the cleaning tool
in his hand. It knocks against a loose
brick, dislodging it.

A THUMP below. Black BELLOWS in pain,
and erupts in a torrent of threats.

Peter reverses direction and starts
climbing again. Almost at the top he
discovers he is bigger than the
chimney opening. He stops to catch his
breath. Not a peep from below.

Peter rubs his nose with his hand and
startles. He scents the air. He looks
down to see a charcoal fire set on the
grate below.

>   PETER
> Oh God, if you can help me,
> help me now!

In the hellish glow, he can see that
the bricks around him have little
mortar between them.

EXT. THE ROOF - DAY

The bricks of the chimney fall in a
CLATTER as Peter bursts through,
flopping down onto the roof. He slips
from under some bricks and scrambles
to his feet. He staggers to the ladder
propped against the roof.

THE ROAD

Peter's running figure disappears over a rise in the road.

THE FIELD

Peter retraces his course across the field by which they came. Before him London stretches in both directions.

A dog BARKS in the distance. Others BARK in response. Peter hesitates and looks back over his shoulder. A coach enters blocking him from view.

As the coach passes, Peter swings up to a perch at the back of the coach. The coach comes to the end of the field and is swallowed up by the city.

EXT. THE BLUE CLOUD INN/COURTYARD - DAY

The sign for the inn CREAKS under the force of a freshening wind, as Peter walks beneath it into the back courtyard. He looks back over his shoulder. Nothing.

Peter makes straight for the stable and to WILL, the stable-boy hard at work sweeping.

> PETER
> Say, Will, is Roger 'bout?

Will stops sweeping.

>   WILL
>   What's a dirty little nigger
>   want with Mr. Morgan?

>   PETER
>   I'm not a dirty nigger. And
>   I'll speak with Roger!

>   WILL
>   He ain't here!

Will goes back to sweeping.

>   PETER
>   When will he be?

Will shrugs his shoulder, then turns
his back on Peter.

AT A WATER PUMP

Peter tries to wash the soot off his
face and hands. Although his hands
come clean, his face remains streaked.

He spots something at the base of the
trough and bends down to retrieve it.

C.U. ON PETER'S HAND

which holds a new pencil. He beams
with joy.

EXT. A COFFEEHOUSE - DAY

Peter, ensconced on a huge hogshead,
doodles with his new-found prize,
oblivious to the HUBBUB around him.

> JERRY (O.S.)
> Look Andrew! It's Liza's
> Peter!

Peter looks up from his work into the face of a happy giant. He jumps to his feet.

> PETER
> Jerry!
>> (seeing Jerry's
>> companion)
> Andrew!

Jerry transfers him from the barrel to his shoulder, and turns to his companion, ANDREW, an athletic man who moves with cat-like grace, a Merry Andrew by trade.

> PETER (CONT'D)
> Have you seen Roger?

> JERRY
> No.
>> (to Andrew)
> Can Peter join us for a
> bite?

Andrew hesitates in thought, then nods his assent.

ACROSS AND DOWN THE STREET

A small crowd has gathered around George, on the corner, preaching. He seems to have cast quite a spell over the crowd. They are quiet, respectful, and intent on his words.

                    GEORGE
          And so, my friends, let us
          reflect for a moment. Who
          are we? What are we that we
          deserve such love? I tell
          you we are nothing. Nothing
          at all. Far from deserving
          such love, we deserve the
          opposite. If we were to get
          what we do deserve, every
          one of us would be bound
          over to prison with no hope
          ever of reprieve. But,
          praise God, that when we are
          repentant, God gives to us
          exactly what we don't
          deserve - forgiveness and
          his loving mercy...

INT. THE COFFEEHOUSE - DAY

A loud, happy commotion fills the
coffeehouse, punctuated by CRIES of
exultation and MOANS of loss.

C.U. A PAIR OF LICE

One "races" down an improvised track.
The other is stock still. A large
thumb squashes the sedentary louse.

BACK TO SCENE

TOOMEY, a muscle-bound sedan-chairman
complains to TINY, a pickpocket.

                    TOOMEY
          Whud you do that for?

> TINY
> It's my bleeding louse. I'll
> have my pleasure I will. If
> this one won't win for me
> I'll get another that will.
> Plenty of 'em around you
> know.

Andrew, Jerry and Peter sit at table
sharing a sizable hunk of bread, and
watching the gambling.

Jerry scratches his head. Andrew moves
close to Jerry, and stares intently at
the back of his head. He picks
something out.

> ANDREW
> Cor... You're a fast one.
> Let's get you entered
> straightway. Jerry, play the
> steward and call the next
> race.

> JERRY
> (banging the table)
> Hear, hear, gen'l'min. The
> Right Hon'rable Andrew Simms
> declares his challenge.

At the announcement, Andrew dances a
jig, and flashes a smile to the
assemblage.

> VOICE FROM THE
> CROWD
> Throw Merry Andrew a copper.

> ANDREW
> I'll pit my steed against
> the current champion.

              TOOMEY
You wouldn't, by chance, be
a-trying to take advantage
of my poor Rosie's spent
condition, now, would ye?

              ANDREW
Certainly not! I believe we
could both come to an
agreeable post time, say, a
quarter hour hence?

              TOOMEY
Done! What you prepared to
wager?

There are cries of "Hear, hear," from
the rest of the men standing around
the table.

              ANDREW
A moment, gentlemen, while I
consult my treasurer.

Andrew and Jerry put their heads
together.

          ANDREW (CONT'D)
How much we got?

              JERRY
One pound and seven. And
mind you, we'll need half of
that to redeem your
trappings from the
pawnbroker. And we need to
do that before we go around
and see Jenny.

              ANDREW
I'm going to bet it all. I'm
feeling lucky.

Jerry takes out a small purse and pours its contents into Andrew's hands.

                    JERRY
          I dunnoh, Andrew, I don't
          think Jenny'd approve of us
          a-gambling with her money.

                    ANDREW
          Leave Jenny to me, Jerry, my
          boy. Win or lose.

The door to the coffeehouse CRASHES open and two bodies fall through onto the floor. George is on the bottom and the second man, SEAN, a street tough, pummels him about the face and chest. The denizens of the coffeehouse quickly gather around the two figures.

                    TOOMEY
          A half crown on the
          clergyman!

                    ANDREW
          My money's for the brawny
          fellow.

George manages to bring his arms up to cover his head and ward off some of the force of the blows. Peter tugs on Jerry's sleeve with a pleading look.

                    JERRY
          Sorry, Andrew, but I can't
          stand by...

Jerry wades into the fray, grabs Sean around the middle and lifts him bodily off of George. ABRAM, an elderly night watchman and a CONSTABLE enter. The constable moves to apprehend Jerry.

George rises from the floor.

> GEORGE
> (indicating the
> attacker)
> No, constable, you want that
> other man. This man is my
> rescuer.

The denizens of the coffeehouse now restrain Sean, pinning his arms to his side and hand him over to the constable.

Abram lends a shoulder to support George. George has him stop before Jerry.

> GEORGE (CONT'D)
> Thank you, sir.

As they pass out into the street, Jerry replies.

> JERRY
> 'Twas nothing. But maybe in
> future you should stay
> inside your church to
> preach.

Andrew has taken a seat at the table and calls to everyone.

> ANDREW
> Post time, gentlemen!

EXT. STREET IN A POOR NEIGHBORHOOD - DAY

Two black cats lap from their reflections in a puddle. They scatter at the sound (o.s.) of a coach.

The coach stops by the puddle in front of a modest house. Abram steps down from the coach.

> ABRAM
> Thanks, George.

> GEORGE
> No. Thank you, my friend. And thank God for your timely arrival.

Abram begins to walk away, then stops.

> ABRAM
> George, could I talk to you about something?

> GEORGE
> I thought something was troubling you.

Abram openly agitated falls silent.

> GEORGE (CONT'D)
> Have courage man, out with it.

> ABRAM
> I have steadfastly resisted corruption on my post as a night watchman...

> GEORGE
> You are to be commended and encouraged.

                    ABRAM
          Encouraged?...by you,
          always, but by my superiors,
          never.

                    GEORGE
          How is that, Abram?

                    ABRAM
          They try to intimidate me
          from seeing and reporting
          certain things. And George,
          I must confess there have
          been times I have gone
          along, more fearful of what
          men say than what God would.
          More fearful, I am ashamed
          to say, of losing my living.

                    GEORGE
          Everyone desiring to live a
          godly life in Christ Jesus
          will face persecution. You
          must steel yourself with
          that truth.

                    ABRAM
          I know, I know...but George,
          I'm so weak...

George reaches an arm to his shoulder
to comfort him.

                    GEORGE
          Rejoice, Abram. These are
          the times when living for
          the Lord, I have found, are
          the most exciting. Remember
          Him who supplies a way out
          of our temptations.

                    ABRAM
Would you advise me to
resign my post?

                    GEORGE
Nay. I am not advising you
one way or the other. It may
very well be the way out.
But be open, the Lord may
call for you to confront
those who tempt you.

                    ABRAM
Surely not! I...I...could
never... I would rather
resign first!

                    GEORGE
Listen, Abram. In all the
issues of life, we
believers, must surrender
our wills to His. And be
obedient.

ANOTHER LONDON STREET

Andrew rides in a sedan chair, waving
regally to passersby. Beside the
chair, Peter walks with a grinning
Jerry who carries a large parcel tied
up with string. Toomey, a disgruntled
look on his face, holds onto the bars
of the sedan chair and maneuvers it
through the crowded street.

                    TOOMEY
Make way! Make way!

THE SEVEN DIALS

A raised platform stands in the center
of the crowded square. JENNY, a baby-
faced woman, stands there alone, her
head and hands locked into a pillory.

Toomey and his sedan chair arrive in
the square, and his cries of "Make
way" intensify. Jerry lends his bulk
to push through the crowd. Toomey and
his PARTNER set the sedan chair down
in front of the platform and Andrew
steps out. He bows to the crowd, they
return the favor by CHEERING.

> JENNY
> About time you got here! You
> promised you'd be here to
> protect me!

Jenny's outburst ignites LAUGHTER.
Andrew mimes a rejected lover,
beseeching his love's forgiveness.

> JENNY (CONT'D)
> Don't you dare toy with me,
> Andrew!

At this Andrew somersaults onto the
stage, landing on his hands and
"walks" over to Jenny, amidst APPLAUSE
from the crowd. He stops in front of
Jenny and smiles up at her.

> ANDREW
> Come on forgive me, Jenny-
> girl.

Jenny swiftly cocks her leg to aim a
kick at Andrew.

                    JENNY
          I'll teach ya to look up my
          dress!

She lets fly with her foot. Andrew
springs back into a tuck and rolls off
of the platform, falling to the ground
out of her sight. Unhurt, he raises a
finger to his lips to caution the
crowd not to give him away, and then
he moans pitifully. Peter GIGGLES, but
Andrew shoots him a stern look. Andrew
motions to him and the others to bend
down to him.

                    ANDREW
             (in a whisper)
          Pretend I'm hurt and keep
          her looking here.

Rising to a crouch he makes his way
around to the back of the platform.
Jerry stands to his feet.

                    JERRY
          Send for a doctor!

Jenny's not convinced, she glares at
Jerry. Toomey motions to his partner,
the other chair-man.

                    TOOMEY
          Go and fetch a doctor, lad.

                    JENNY
          He'll need a doctor and
          that's for sure, when I get
          out o' here!

But she begins to soften.

> PETER
> Aunt Jenny I'm afraid you've hurt him real bad! He's bleeding terribly!

Andrew climbs the platform from in back, and crosses to Jenny.

> JENNY
> Andrew! Andrew! I forgive you. Forgive me!

Andrew swings around to the front and kisses her on the lips. The crowd relishes the spectacle.

Jenny squirms under the rough kiss and finally breaks free, gasping for breath.

> JENNY (CONT'D)
> You...you...

> ANDREW
> Jenny! Jenny! Calm down, you'll do yourself a hurt.

Jerry and Peter climb onto the platform.

> JERRY
> We were just having some fun, Jen.

> JENNY
> (looking at Andrew)
> Mocking me, you mean!

She looks to Jerry and sees the parcel.

                    JENNY
          I'm surprised you didn't put
          your costume on and do it up
          right.

                    ANDREW
          Now, Jen, admit it, you'd be
          just as mad if we didn't pay
          you any attention.

                    JERRY
          Besides Andrew didn't have
          time, we only just came from
          the pawnshop with them...

Andrew gives Jerry the eye in an
attempt to stop him from letting the
cat out of the bag.

                    JERRY (CONT'D)
          ...and you know we have lots
          left over from what we
          won...

                    JENNY
          What? You won what!!??

                    ANDREW
          Just some little winnings
          from a bet.

                    JENNY
          You...you made a bet? How
          much was it Jerry?

                    JERRY
          Just all we had.

At this Jenny loses it again.

                    JENNY
          All? Everything?

> ANDREW
> Now, Jenny, everything's all
> right. Don't...

> JENNY
> You took my money and bet
> it...

> ANDREW
> But we won, Jenny, we won!

Jenny falls deathly silent, her lips
in a grim line.

> ANDREW (CONT'D)
> Don't carry on that way,
> Jen. Look, Jerry and I have
> a chance at a job.

He holds up an advertisement.

> ANDREW (CONT'D)
> A mountebank is looking for
> a "Merry Andrew"--

> JERRY
> Aye, and a strongman too. Me
> and Andrew are headed there
> now.

> ANDREW
> Shut up, Jerry, before you
> bury the both of us. Pass me
> that other parcel.

Jerry gives him an even larger parcel
from which Andrew takes out a
beautiful dress.

> ANDREW (CONT'D)
> There, my love, the very one
> (MORE)

                    ANDREW (CONT'D)
          you've been pining for. You
          see, I haven't forgotten
          you.

Delight transforms Jenny's face.

                    JENNY
          Oh, Andrew...

                    ANDREW
          And so milady, if I have
          your permission, and with
          Peter on guard...
               (Peter nods)
          I shall go in search of our
          fortune.

LATER

The afternoon finds the crowds
dispersed looking for other
amusements. Though "on guard," Peter
busily sketches. He chances to look up
and notices a tall figure just leaving
the square.

                    PETER
               (breathless whisper)
          Roger!

He turns to look at Jenny. Jenny, her
hair hanging in sweaty strings, dozes
on her feet.

Peter fights off a spasm of guilt,
pockets his drawing things and sets
out again on his quest for Roger.

LONE SIDE STREET

Ahead Peter spots an odd duo torturing a dog. One is the ruffian, SEAN, at liberty, and the other EGBERT, by his dress, an aristocrat. Egbert has the dog wedged under his arm.

                    SEAN
          Hold him still!

Sean struggles to insert a metal rod up the dog's anus.

                    ALICE
          Let go of my dog! Let go!

The young girl runs up and grabs Egbert's leg and tries to shake her pet loose.

Sean drops the rod, steps around to Alice, pulls her from Egbert and pushes her to the ground. She screams.

                    SEAN
          Shut up! Or you're next!

At her scream, Peter comes running.

Sean has returned to his "business". Both he and Egbert have their backs towards Peter. He bowls into Sean's legs, pushing him against Egbert. Egbert drops the dog.

The dog snarls at his tormentor and lunges at him.

Egbert streaks down the alley, barely ahead of the charging dog. Sean picks up the rod and threatens Peter with it. But unknown to him a new figure enters from behind.

>   ROGER MORGAN
>   Still the bully, eh, Sean?

Sean lowers the rod and turns.

Roger smiles broadly. His greatcoat
lies open revealing a brace of pistols
in his belt.

Sean backs away slowly, then turns and
runs.

Roger helps Alice to her feet.

>   ROGER
>   I trust you are well,
>   miss...?

>   ALICE
>   Alice. I'm fine, now,
>   thanks.

Roger turns his attention to Peter,
who is at his side in an instant.

>   ROGER
>   Are you hurt, Peter?

>   PETER
>   No, sir.

>   ROGER
>   That was a mighty brave
>   thing you did.

>   ALICE
>   Oh, yes!

Peter blushes beet red.

                    PETER
          'Tweren't nothing you
          wouldn't do, Roger.

Roger looks at the two.

                    ROGER
          You both look like you could
          do with a meal.

Alice's dog returns with a ripped
piece of cloth in his jaws. He
deposits it at her feet. She looks up
to Roger.

                    ALICE
          Thank'ee kindly, sir, but
          Codger and I need to be
          going.

                    ROGER
          Well, then, Peter?

                    PETER
          Oh! Yes!

EXT. THE BLUE CLOUD INN/COURTYARD -
NIGHT

From out of the inn wafts the chorus
to the tune, "St. George he was for
England". At a table in the courtyard,
Roger draws the attention of all about
him like iron filings to a magnet.

                    ROGER
          There I was astride my
          steed, with my pistols aimed
          at the black heart of a fat,
          puking tailor. I could feel
          him a-quaking in his boots.

                    TINY
          (aside to others)
A-squirting in his breeches,
he means.

                    ROGER
God bless my soul, says I to
myself, as I can see a heavy
weight beneath his shirt.
I'll have your toll before I
see you on your way, I says.
And he screws up his
sheepish eyes to me and
bleats out, "If it please
your honor, I surrender all,
but could you find it within
ye to humor me. I would be
much the scorn of my brother
tailors if I were thought to
have given up without a
fight. All I propose, is a
little deception." And here
he doffs his hat and asks me
to discharge my pistol into
it, to show as proof, he
says, of his courage.

Peter leans forward, enraptured by the
story.

                    ROGER (CONT'D)
Well, being myself ever
willing to oblige my
customers, I fired not one
but both my pistols through
the crown of his hat. And
what do you think? Out from
under his shirt he whips a
pistol of his own, and just
stands there a-grinning at
me. To tell you the truth, I
was speechless at his
perfidy.

                    PETER
            So...what happened?

                    ROGER
            I whipped that flintlock out
            o' his hand and hit him o'er
            the head with it.
                (he winks at Peter)
            Then I relieved him of that
            afore mentioned weight and
            took that pledge of his
            courage to boot.

At this, he holds up the hat, twirling
it on his finger.

MR. BLACK

From the lane that enters the
courtyard, Mr. Black watches. He turns
and walks swiftly away.

BACK TO SCENE

Will, now a server, brings out
trenchers with mounds of steaming beef
and places them at their table. The
other men depart leaving Roger, Tiny,
and Peter to their meal. Roger motions
to Will that he must also serve Peter.
Chagrined, Will does so with a wary
eye on Roger.

                    TINY
                (to Peter)
            How be the trade, do you
            find it...looking up?

Tiny elbows Roger at his jest. But
Peter downcasts his eyes.

                                    ROGER
                     Well, then, run away is it?
                     Look at me my lad. 'Tis a
                     serious business.

                                    PETER
                     But you ran away from your
                     'prenticeship.

                                    TINY
                     Aye, designs on his master's
                     horse and equipage.

A CHIME SOUNDS. Tiny takes out a fine
gold-cased watch. He winds the stem
and holds it up to his ear. Peter
watches with interest, which Tiny
slyly appreciates and hands him the
piece to admire.

                                    TINY (CONT'D)
                     Handsome, don't you think?
                     Would you like to have one
                     of your very own?

                                    PETER
                     Oh, could I, Tiny?

                                    ROGER
                     Tiny, you're not a-going to
                     'prentice Peter to your
                     craft.

                                    TINY
                     I dunnoh Roger, I kinda feel
                     Peter would be good at it.

                                    ROGER
                          (to Peter)
                     Pay no heed to him. I would
                     see you raised up to a
                     quality trade, I would.

Roger chases his last bite of meat around his trencher with his fork. He spears it and raises it up in a toast.

> ROGER (CONT'D)
> To the good life, and the knight-errantry of the road.

> TINY
> Worth taking a ride on the three-legged mare?

Roger finishes his morsel and replies.

> ROGER
> Aye! It be the only business worth dancing at the end of a rope for.

> TINY
> (sarcastic)
> A quality trade? A better one in your estimation for the boy here?

Peter looks up from gnawing a bone.

> PETER
> (standing)
> Oh, yes, Roger, could you take me on as 'prentice?

> ROGER
> No, no, my young sirrah. You are much too young. I must insist you make all haste back to your master.

> PETER
> But, Roger. I can't. I caused a brick to fall on his head.

                        TINY
            I wouldn't worry on that
            score, Master Black's head
            be harder than most.

                        PETER
            And I destroyed the Bishop's
            chimney. No, I can't go
            back.

At this, Roger rests his chin in one
hand and squints one eye in thought.

Black, the CONSTABLE and THREE MEN and
the FAT TAILOR sweep around from the
lane into the courtyard.

                        BLACK
            There he is! My runaway
            'prentice.

                        FAT TAILOR
            In faith, it's the man who
            robbed me!

The body of men rushes forward.

                        CONSTABLE
            Keep the peace, gentlemen,
            and hand over the boy.

Before they reach the group, Roger
lifts Peter from the table, and
catapults him up onto the second story
of the inn behind them.

                        ROGER
            Run, Petey, my lad! Run!

Black charges into the inn, but he
collides with Will, and ends up
wearing someone's dinner.

Roger bolts for the stable across the courtyard, and Tiny tries to run interference for him. The fat tailor bowls him over and tackles Roger.

Stunned, Peter looks down from a little balcony. But as the constable sends the other three men into the inn, he climbs through a window.

INT. THE BLUE CLOUD INN/SECOND FLOOR/ END ROOM

Peter charges through the darkness crashing into things upsetting crockery and furniture. He gains the door and passes by it into...

THE BLUE CLOUD INN/SECOND FLOOR/ HALLWAY

A general HEW and CRY ascends from below stairs. Peter hears heavy FOOTFALLS on the backstairs, so he races down the hallway to the front. His hand on the latch to a door of a front room, he pauses and looks back to see Black and the three men reach the top of the stairs.

                    PETER
          O, God, help this door to be
          unlocked!

Peter lifts the latch and pushes into the room, slamming the door behind.

THE BLUE CLOUD INN/SECOND FLOOR/FRONT
ROOM

is dark and Peter hears someone
stirring in the bed at the center of
the room.

> WOMAN'S VOICE
> (waking)
> Who's there?

Peter dives under her bed, just as
Black and company come rushing into
the room.

> WOMAN'S VOICE
> (CONT'D)
> (screams)
> Ahh! Robbers! Thieves!
> Murderers!

As two of the men go around to the
window, the woman grabs the chamber-
pot from beneath her bed and throws it
at the heads of her tormenters. In the
confusion Peter rabbits through the
legs of Black and the third man. Black
lunges for him, but only comes up with
Peter's shoe. The door bangs shut.

PETER

Clambers down the stairs in front and
shoots out into the street.

EXT. THE BLUE CLOUD INN/COURTYARD

The constable restrains Roger,
awaiting the outcome from within.
Tiny, out of the constable's sight,
slides away from the group, and

tiptoes to the stable.

INT. THE BLUE CLOUD INN/STABLE

Tiny pauses at the back door, turns
and looks towards the courtyard.

                    TINY
          What to do? What...to...do?

He wrings his hands. He steps toward
the front and stops. A horse NEIGHS.
Inspiration dawns.

EXT. THE BLUE CLOUD INN/COURTYARD

A horse bolts from the stable. Roger
jerks himself from the grip of the
constable and runs for the horse,
leaps onto its bare back and makes for
the lane, just at the instant that
Black and the three men return
blocking the exit. Roger's horse
rears, throwing him to the ground.

STREET CORNER

Peter, bent double and leaning against
a building, gasps for breath. He looks
anxiously back down the street. A
SCRAPING NOISE from in back of him
brings Peter bolt upright. Jacob, a
night watchman, limps around the
corner dragging a short ladder. Both
are surprised to encounter one
another. Jacob recovers first.

                              JACOB
               The devil take me, you gave
               me a start. Where did you
               come from?

Peter makes no reply.

                              JACOB (CONT'D)
               Well, step aside and let me
               light the lamp, I want to
               get back to my bed.

Peter complies, and watches while he
lights the lamp.

                              JACOB (CONT'D)
               There. Now you won't scare a
               body.

Peter takes off around the corner and
runs smack into a wall of flesh. It is
Jerry walking in convoy with Andrew.
Jerry's arms go around the lad, but
Peter, eyes shut, drums on his chest
to be let go.

                              JERRY
               Hold on there, me lad. It be
               your friend Jerry, you're a-
               beating.

Peter stops flailing and Jerry puts
him down.

                              ANDREW
               I thought we left you with
               Jenny?

                    PETER
          You did, but...
               (he looks back)
          Roger! The constable! I
          gotta...

A stab of fear passes over Jerry's
face.

                    ANDREW
          Roger's big enough to take
          care of himself. Right now
          let's see to you.

Jerry notices that Peter is without a
shoe.

                    JERRY
          Ho. Peter, you lack a shoe.
          Climb up and I'll carry ya.

Jerry swings him up onto his back and
Peter rides there piggy-back.

                    JERRY (CONT'D)
          We got those jobs, Petey.

                    ANDREW
          You'd better stay with us,
          lad, until we can sort
          through things.
               (he studies Peter)
          First thing let's wash you
          up.

                    PETER
          Wash me?! I already washed!

EXT. THE GLOBE AND URINAL INN/
COURTYARD - NIGHT

Peter's head resembles a rock in a

streambed as Jerry finishes pouring a
bucket of water over it. Andrew
arrives with some rags and begins
rubbing him dry.

> PETER
> Not so hard, you're rubbing
> my skin off!

> ANDREW
> Hold still! I'm almost done.

Andrew scowls at the now blackened
rags. He wads them into a lump and
tosses them out into the courtyard.

Jerry hefts him over to the step and
the group enters the Globe and Urinal.

INT. THE GLOBE AND URINAL INN/ANDREW
AND JERRY'S ROOM - DAY

Peter sits in the window, drawing on
the sill. Outside in the street
Gabriel passes by.

C.U. OF HIS SKETCH

Another comic rendition of Mr. Black
looks up from the window sill. Peter's
pencil blackens his teeth in.

BACK TO SCENE

> GABRIEL (O.S.)
> Chimneys! Chimneys swept!
> Chimneys! Chimneys swept!

Peter freezes. Then, as he drops from

the window to the floor, the door to the room swings open and Jerry saunters in.

> JERRY
> Ho, Peter! What's all this?

> PETER
> I just heard Gabriel a-crying up the street, and I thought Mr. Black...

> JERRY
> Don't you worry about that blackguard, not while I'm around.
> (He takes out some shoes)
> Here, I've something for you.

Before Peter can say thanks, he goes to the corner of the room and opens a trunk.

> JERRY (CONT'D)
> No need to thank me. Andrew sent me back to retrieve this anyway.

He holds up a pneumatic bottle.

> JERRY (CONT'D)
> The professor wants Andrew to do his sneezing routine this afternoon.

He places the apparatus in his haversack.

> JERRY (CONT'D)
> I got some bad news, lad.
> (MORE)

> JERRY (CONT'D)
> The news about town is that
> your friend Roger is taken.

>> PETER
>> No!

Collapsing on the bed, he physically
shrinks into a shell. Jerry touches
his shoulder to comfort him.

> PETER (CONT'D)
> (in a small voice)
> Do you know where he is?

> JERRY
> Newgate, I suppose. Do you
> want to come and be with
> Andrew and me?

>> PETER
>> No, no thanks.

Jerry turns to leave. About to close
the door, he adds.

> JERRY
> You better stay here, then.

No sooner does the door shut than
Peter has his new shoes on. He stares
wistfully out the window at Newgate
Prison off in the distance, then up at
the heavens.

> PETER (O.S.)
> God. Is it 'cause I did
> something wrong?

EXT. NEWGATE STREET - DAY

A vicious looking dog paces in front
of the prison where a GATEKEEPER
stands guard. Peter watches from
across the street.

A passel of PROSTITUTES come to a stop
in front of the prison gates. They are
accompanied by Egbert and three other
potential customers. Peter perks up
when he sees LIZA, his mother,
approaching from behind the group.

>   PROSTITUTE ONE
>   (to Liza)
>   Lost, dearie?

>   EGBERT
>   Halloa. What have we here?

>   PROSTITUTE TWO
>   A fair ways from home, ain't
>   ya, Liza?

>   EGBERT
>   Have you no manners? You
>   simply must introduce me.

Prostitute Two grips Egbert's arm
possessively.

>   PROSTITUTE TWO
>   You don't want to have
>   anything to do with her
>   kind.

>   PROSTITUTE ONE
>   Aye, she consorts with
>   Frenchmen.

They laugh. Liza storms past and

doesn't look back.

Peter crosses the street to join her, picking his way carefully among the coaches, carts and men pushing wheelbarrows.

> PETER
> Momma! Wait!

Liza turns surprised.

> LIZA
> Peter! What are you doing here?

> PETER
> I want to visit my father, too.

> LIZA
> How many times do I gotta tell you he's not your father?

> PETER
> But you told me once he could be.

> LIZA
> Well, he's not, and more importantly he doesn't want to be! Not after what you've done.

At this Peter's demeanor collapses.

> PETER
> That's why I gotta talk to him. I gotta tell him I'm sorry.

                    LIZA
        Sorry?! You'd be lucky--

                    PETER
        --Please, mama, I gotta...

She studies him a second.

                    LIZA
                (exasperated)
        Come with me.

She takes him by the hand and marches
over to the entrance.

The mastiff pacing in front snarls.
The pair skirt around the dog and the
gatekeeper emerges.

                    GATEKEEPER
        Top o' the morning, Mrs.

                    LIZA
        Good day, sir.

As the two disappear from sight,
Egbert strides up to the gatekeeper.

                    EGBERT
        Pardon me, sir. I believe I
        know that lady who just now
        entered.

                    GATEKEEPER
        You mean Mrs. Morgan?

                    EGBERT
        Yes, then, it was my Liza.

                    GATEKEEPER
        Your Liza? Why, she be here
        to visit her husband.

                    EGBERT
          You misread me, sir. She is
          a friend. I am only
          surprised to hear of her
          misfortune.

                    GATEKEEPER
          Misfortune, aye. But more so
          for her husband, for she'll
          soon be a widow.

At this Egbert smiles, which the
gatekeeper notices and it sets him
CACKLING.

INT. NEWGATE PRISON/ROGER'S CELL - DAY

Roger and his cell-mate BOB TRICKETT
sit at a table in the center of the
room, playing cards.

Bob plays his last card, a Queen of
Hearts, with a flourish.

                    BOB
          My trick, and my game!

Roger looks sourly at the small pile
of cards before him.

                    ROGER
          Bad run o' luck. I need to
          quit while I still have
          money for my keep.

                    BOB
          Come on Roger, neither of us
          will be able to spend it
          where we're a-going.

Bob leans back in his chair and

stretches his legs onto the table.

                    ROGER
          I got plenty o' things to
          spend it on now. I've got my
          lady to consider.

                    BOB
          You've got it all backwards.
          It's them outside that needs
          to look after us.

He sweeps his hat off of the table and
covers his heart.

                    BOB (CONT'D)
          The least they can do for
          the nearly departed. Heh,
          heh, heh, ha, ha.

EXT. NEWGATE PRISON/THE PRESS YARD -
DAY

Liza stops at the entrance to the
Governor's wing.

                    LIZA
          Wait here, Peter. I'll see
          if Roger'll see you.

                    PETER
          But, Mama...

                    LIZA
          Don't "mama" me, saucebox!
          Sit here and wait.

He acquiesces and sits on the steps.

INT. NEWGATE PRISON/ROGER'S CELL - DAY

Roger and Bob turn towards the door at its opening. A TURNKEY ushers Liza in.

                    ROGER
          Liza!

Bob picks his coat up from the chair and throws it on.

                    BOB
          My compliments to you, my
          lady.

Bob takes her hand and kisses it. She answers with a curtsy.

                    LIZA
          Please Bob, there is no
          necessity for you to leave.

The turnkey stands looking bored.

                    BOB
          Ah, but Liza, there is the
          most urgent necessity for me
          to leave, though perhaps not
          my own.

Bob bows and then strides out, the turnkey in tow. Liza flies into Roger's arms.

EXT. NEWGATE PRISON/THE PRESS YARD

Peter still sits on the steps.

C.U. PETER'S SKETCH

Peter puts the finishing touches to

his drawing of Roger.

At the sound of STEPS, Peter rises.

> BOB
> Halloa, young man. What are
> ye about? Not up before the
> Ol' Bailey, I hope?

> PETER
> No. Sir. I'm a-waitin' for
> my mama.

> BOB
> And what d'ye got there?

Peter quickly folds his drawing, and
makes to put it away.

> BOB (CONT'D)
> Have no fear, I may be in
> Newgate, but I am no robber
> of children.

The turnkey passes them.

> BOB (CONT'D)
> Turnkeys, yes. Children. No.

Peter hands the drawing to him. Bob
looks at it and then back at Peter
with surprise.

> BOB (CONT'D)
> Why, that's me mate, Roger.
> You have a fine hand, me
> lad. (A beat) Ye must be
> Liza's boy, Peter. Roger has
> told me all about you.

Peter colors and casts his eyes down.

                    PETER
          Is he...is he angry with me?

                    BOB
          Angry? Angry? What cause
          would ol' Roger have to be
          angry with you?

                    PETER
          He...he hasn't told you that
          it was on account of me that
          he got caught?

                    BOB
          Heh, heh, heh, ha, ha!
          You...you got ol' Roger
          caught?

                    PETER
          Aye.

                    BOB
          Roger no more holds you
          accountable for that
          than...than he would me.

Peter brightens.

                    BOB (CONT'D)
          No, sir. He has nothing but
          kind words for yourself. Let
          me show you around and then
          we'll have you pay your
          respects.

NEWGATE PRISON/NEXT TO THE STONE HOLD

                    BOB
          'At's the Stone Hold, Pete,
          me boy. 'Tis where they keep
                    (MORE)

                    BOB (CONT'D)
          the women prisoners. Not
          much to look at, mind you,
          give me a lady of quality
          any day.

They round a corner and Bob stops in
front of a low, forbidding doorway.
And then begins to go on.

                    PETER
          What's in there?

                    BOB
          'At's Jack Ketch's
          "kitchen." Not a place ye
          wanna be.

                    PETER
          Jack Ketch? The executioner?

Excited, Peter lingers and edges
nearer the door.

                    PETER (CONT'D)
          Do ye think he might be
          hereabouts?

Bob looks back just in time to see
Peter disappear through the doorway.

                    BOB
          Peter!

INT. NEWGATE PRISON/JACK KETCH'S
KITCHEN - DAY

Gloom shrouds the room, even though a
fire burns on a large central hearth,
its flickering light only serves to
illuminate the irons and chains
hanging on the walls. Peter,

trembling, picks up a leg iron and
then lets it fall against the wall
with a CLANK. "JACK KETCH," emerges
from the back of the room, carrying a
half knotted noose.

> KETCH
> Hey, there, boy! What d'ye
> want?

Peter, his eyes glued on the noose,
stands frozen to the spot.

> KETCH (CONT'D)
> Come on! Speak up!

Bob comes to his rescue.

> BOB
> Come on, Peter, we must be
> off! Beg your pardon, Mr.
> Ketch.

Bob drags Peter by the arm out into
the light of the Press Yard.

Ketch smirks and returns to the back
of the room. There he joins THOMAS
PURNEY, the prison cleric, at the
table.

> KETCH
> Devil take 'em all, heh
> Tummas?

> PURNEY
> Quite right. Absolutely.

Ketch tipsily takes his seat, picks up
a bottle and refills two cups. He
resumes tying the noose.

                    KETCH
          We'll be a-seeing him next
          Tyburn Fair, him and that
          other highwayman, Roger
          Morgan. They'll pay dear for
          a sweet dance, I should say.

He finishes the noose and holds it up
for inspection and gives a couple
pulls to test its strength.

                    PURNEY
          Let us not go counting our
          chickens before they're
          hatched.

                    KETCH
          I'd be willing to venture
          you a guinea that we'll be
          a-collecting from them
          before they leave this life.

Purney picks up his pipe from the
table and draws a puff.

                    PURNEY
          Let's make it two, then,
          seeing you're so confident.

Ketch raises his drink in agreement.

EXT. NEWGATE STREET - DAY

Across from the prison Egbert watches
the comings and goings. Sean taps him
on the shoulder.

                    SEAN
          Ah. Master Egbert, I see you
          are renewing your studies in
          the Law.

Startled Egbert wheels around.

> EGBERT
> Oh, it's just you.

Egbert turns his attention immediately back to the entrance of Newgate.

> EGBERT (CONT'D)
> I wish you wouldn't call me by my Christian name.

> SEAN
> And what do you prefer to be called by, Eggie?

> EGBERT
> Not now, Sean!

> SEAN
> Ah! 'Tis a woman, then, isn't it?

Egbert takes his gaze off of the prison and levels it at Sean.

> EGBERT
> Alright, yes. Now, please be quiet!

EXT. NEWGATE PRISON/ROGER'S CELL - DAY

> PETER
> Can't we go right in?

> BOB
> A gentleman never enters unbidden. One must first knock.

Bob raps the door with ceremony. Roger opens it.

                    ROGER
          Peter!

Roger picks the lad up and carries him
on his shoulder into the room. Bob
follows.

INT. NEWGATE PRISON/ROGER'S CELL - DAY

                    ROGER
          Look, Liza, see who's come
          to visit.
               (He looks up to Peter)
          Well, I am glad one of us is
          at liberty.

Liza winces.

                    PETER
          I have something for you,
          Roger.

Peter reaches into his pocket and
takes out his sketch. Roger seats him
on the table and takes the proffered
paper. He studies it.

                    ROGER
          A most handsome drawing.

Clearly touched, he folds and places
it in his shirt. He pats the spot.

                    ROGER (CONT'D)
          I shall treasure it, Peter,
          my lad, as long as I live.

Liza sobs once. Roger runs to her
side.

>   ROGER (CONT'D)
> There I go again, unmindful
> of my tongue. 'Twill all be
> right, just find Tiny, he'll
> know what to do.
>   (To Peter)
> I think it time for you to
> escort your mother out.
>   (To Liza)
> Have courage, my love.

He raises her to her feet. Peter comes
to her side to assist. Roger and Liza
embrace, then part. Peter takes her
hand and they turn to leave. At the
door Peter lets go of her hand,
returns to Roger, stands as tall as he
can, then bows.

>   PETER
> If there is anything I can
> do...

Roger bows in return. They depart.

EXT. FLEET STREET - DAY

The street bustles with activity.
Egbert and Sean hang back but keep
Peter and Liza in view.

From across the street a tenor voice
croons the words to "The Lady Falls".
The singer, PHILLIP-IN-THE-TUB, a
legless man sits on a short wooden
platform that doubles as his legs,
with one hand he touches the ground to
steady himself and in the other are
his wares, penny broadsheets. As Liza
passes, he changes his tune.

                        PHILLIP-IN-THE-TUB
          Li-ah-za, oho, my Li-ah-za.

His audience TITTERS. Liza turns and
shouts at him.

                        LIZA
          The answer is still "NO,"
          Phillip!

She bolts, yanking Peter with her.
Sean and Egbert wade through the
bystanders with a superior air. Sean
snatches the penny broadsheets from
Phillip and tosses them into the air,
and then pushes him off of his
platform.

                        EGBERT
          You should show better
          manners when in the presence
          of a lady.

Those nearby MURMUR in disapproval,
but the sight of Egbert fingering his
sword hilt holds them in check.
Phillip pushes himself back on his
platform. He calls after the departing
duo.

                        PHILLIP-IN-THE-TUB
          I'll swear out a warrant
          agin ye!

Sean and Egbert don't even look back,
but turn to one another and laugh.

                        EGBERT
          Zauns! The cheek of some
          beggars.

Egbert skips ahead and accosts Liza.

                    EGBERT (CONT'D)
          Lord Hawksmoor, at your
          service, milady. My soul was
          pained to see you treated in
          such a wretched manner by
          such a low fellow, Mrs.
          Morgan.

Egbert takes her hand to kiss it, but
she snatches it back.

                    LIZA
          If indeed, you are a
          gentleman, you will not
          force your courtesy where it
          is not welcome.

This brings a smile to Sean's face, as
he has now come up beside his friend.

                    EGBERT
          Listen, both you and I know
          you are a common whore. And
          if that is how you want to
          be treated I shall oblige.

                    PETER
          Leave my mother alone!

                    EGBERT
               (To Sean)
          I thought you were going to
          handle the brat.

Before Sean can reach for Peter, a
hand grips him by the back of the
neck. A second hand grips Egbert
likewise, and they are lifted bodily
from the ground. The hands smack the
two men's heads together and they fall
in a heap at Jerry's feet.

Jerry picks up his haversack.

> JERRY
> 'Twere best you both come
> with me to Covent Garden.

> LIZA
> That's where we were going.
> > (She rises on tiptoe and
> > kisses his cheek)
> Thanks, Jerry, for coming to
> our rescue.

He blushes with embarrassment, and
when she takes his arm to hurry them
along, he is not a little pleased.

EXT. COVENT GARDEN - DAY

From center stage, the mountebank, DR.
CORBIN, makes his pitch. His audience
fills the front, three-deep. Peter,
Liza and Jerry squeeze into the back.

> DR. CORBIN
> And this small miracle in a
> bottle, this marvel of the
> pharmacists' art, I am
> making available to you for
> a pittance. For I have
> purposed not to profit at
> the misery of my fellow
> creatures, but seek with all
> my heart to relieve their
> suffering.

> JERRY
> > (Pipes up)
> Oh, yeah? Show us this
> miracle!

The PEOPLE around him SHOUT in agreement.

> DR. CORBIN
> Merry Andrew! Where are you, fool?

On cue, Andrew emerges from the booth at the back of the stage and gallops over to the mountebank, to the delight of the assemblage. He stands beside the mountebank and wipes his nose first on one sleeve, then on the other.

> ANDREW
> Yes, Master?

> DR. CORBIN
> Here, fool. Some elixir for your cold.

> ANDREW
> No, thank you, Master.

He returns to wiping his nose.

> DR. CORBIN
> Here! I order you to drink some.

> JERRY
> Make him drink it!

Peter looks up at Jerry. Jerry bends down to lend him his ear. He straightens with a smile, takes out a coin and slips it to him. With a wink and a jerk of his head, Jerry motions him to move down to the front. Peter eagerly burrows to the front.

> DR. CORBIN (O.S.)
> Come now, Andrew. You
> wouldn't want to disappoint
> anyone here would you?

> ANDREW (O.S.)
> No, I don't want to
> disappoint anyone, including
> myself.

Peter's head bobs up at the front of
the stage.

> DR. CORBIN
> I can see we are going to
> have to persuade Andrew that
> it's all for his own good.

As the mountebank speaks, Andrew lifts
the quack's coattail and wipes his
nose on it. LAUGHTER ripples through
the crowd.

> JERRY
> Let's see you take it
> Andrew!

Out of Andrew's view, the mountebank
takes a pinch of pepper from a tin. He
turns and blows it into Andrew's face.

Andrew's face scrunches up into a
grotesque mask, and winds up for a
sneeze.

> ANDREW
> Ah.... Ah.... Ah.... Ah....

Andrew clasps his hands over his mouth
and dashes for the booth.

INT. DR. CORBIN'S BOOTH

NICKY, servant to the mountebank, a
beefy teenage boy, helps Andrew into a
harness with the pneumatic bottle, as
Andrew takes a sip of water and a
pinch of snuff.

EXT. DR. CORBIN'S STAGE

Andrew emerges and charges the crowd.
He stops at the edge and lets fly his
sneeze, spraying a good number. The
crowd ROARS.

Andrew falls backward on his butt as
though propelled in reaction to his
sneeze. The plunger on the pneumatic
bottle depresses, sending a steady
stream out into the audience. He
blinks in disbelief.

                    ANDREW
          Master! Master! Quick, give
          me the nostrum before I
          explode!

Andrew walks over to him on his knees.

                    DR. CORBIN
          One dose, not even a full
          bottle should fix you up.

Andrew takes the cup and drinks. In a
second he leaps to his feet and
somersaults around the stage,
proclaiming his cure.

                    JERRY
          I'll take two bottles.

                    PETER
          Give me one!

The mountebank stoops to Peter and
hands him a bottle in exchange for the
coin. He pats him on the head.

Many now crowd nearer, money in hand.
Nicky comes forward with additional
bottles.

Jerry, waving at him from the crowd,
catches Andrew's eye. Andrew signals
him to meet around the back.

BACK OF THE BOOTH

Jerry waits with Liza and Peter when
Andrew emerges through the flap.

                    ANDREW
          About time you got back!

The mountebank emerges too.

                    DR. CORBIN
          No time for words now,
          Andrew. I'll take those
          ingredients, Jerry.

Jerry hands the sack up to him and he
disappears back into the booth.

                    ANDREW
          I hope your memory doesn't
          cost us this job.

                    JERRY
          But, Andrew...

LIZA
Jerry stopped to rescue
Peter and me from two rakes.

The mountebank sticks his head out.

DR. CORBIN
I could use some help here,
you two. We're losing money
as you're standing there.

He disappears as quickly as he
appeared.

JERRY
We better get in there,
Andrew.

ANDREW
You just remember, it wasn't
my fault.

Jerry just shrugs his shoulders, signs
to Liza to wait, and falls in behind
Andrew.

LIZA
Peter, you stay with Jerry
and Andrew. I'm going to
find Tiny.

LIZA

plants herself in the now empty area
in front of the mountebank's stage and
looks out over the square. She scans
it from one side to the other. She
sees Tiny in the opposite corner.

Before Liza reaches him a SMALL BOY
walks by him, stoops and puts

something in a sack by his feet and speeds away.

> LIZA
> Business good, Tiny?

> TINY
> Too good to stop and chat, lass. It's not everyday one gets the best corner.

His eyes flitter around the square while he talks to her.

> LIZA
> Roger needs your help.

> TINY
> I tried to help ol' Roger, but naught come of it. I think your best bet is to buy off that tailor that swore 'gainst him.

> LIZA
> I've tried but he won't forswear his charge. He's out for Roger's blood.

> TINY
> Well, then that's all there is for it, ol' Roger ain't no Jack Sheppard.

> LIZA
> That's true, but sure there's someone in London who can get him out.

Tiny ceases his surveillance of the square and focuses on Liza.

> TINY
> Now you're talking deep
> matters, lass.
> Dangerous..and expensive..

> LIZA
> ..I can get some money. Just
> tell me how much and what
> else I need to do.

Tiny stares thoughtfully.

> TINY
> Aye. But you'll have to
> leave the doing to me.
> Dealing with the Ratcatcher
> is dangerous.

DR. CORBIN'S STAGE

Jerry unhooks a corner of the curtain
that makes up the booth and hands a
section to Andrew.

> PETER
> Do you think I could do what
> I did for money?

> ANDREW
> Maybe so, maybe not. Help us
> get these things back to the
> doctor's and we'll talk.

Peter pitches in to help them.

EXT. DR. CORBIN'S HOUSE - DAY

Jerry and the wagoneer grapple with
the team to maneuver them into the
stable to unload. Andrew helps Peter
down and leads him into the house.

EXT./INT. DR. CORBIN'S HOUSE

Nicky opens the door to them.

>   ANDREW
> I want to see the doctor
> about a job for my friend
> here.

Andrew pushes Peter forward. Nicky
looks Peter up and down.

>   NICKY
> Come this way.

DR. CORBIN'S SITTING-ROOM

Nicky ushers them in. Flasks and
bottles line the shelves on one side
of the room. A large leather-bound
book lies open on the table in the
center of the room, flanked by jars
filled with diseased organs floating
in clear liquid.

>   NICKY
> Wait here, I'll announce you
> to the Doctor.

He knocks on the bedchamber door,
enters and closes it behind him.

Peter examines a putrid looking liver
in one of the jars, he grimaces in
disgust. Nicky returns with Dr.
Corbin.

>   DR. CORBIN
> Works like a charm. If they
> aren't sick--

                    ANDREW
          --make them think they're
          sick.

                    DR. CORBIN
          Spoken like a true member of
          the "fraternity."

                    ANDREW
          And may I introduce to you a
          lad who'd like to join our
          "fraternity."

Dr. Corbin gives his full attention to
Peter, putting on a thoughtful,
judicial face.

                    DR. CORBIN
          Tell me, what can you do?

                    PETER
          I can draw.

He takes out one of his drawings to
show him, but Dr. Corbin waves it off.

                    DR. CORBIN
          Can you sing a song? Or play
          the fool?

                    ANDREW
          He can shill.

                    DR. CORBIN
          I've got Jerry for that.

                    ANDREW
          You know, he could run
          errands. That would keep
          Jerry free for more
          important things.

Dr. Corbin suddenly taken with the thought, nods in agreement.

> DR. CORBIN
> Let's shake on it. You'll begin tomorrow. The boys'll familiarize you with my wares and our routines.

EXT. DR. CORBIN'S HOUSE - DAY

Peter and Andrew float down the steps.

> ANDREW
> What I tell you, signs of things to come. Sweet Dame Fortune is smiling.

INT. DR. CORBIN'S SITTING-ROOM - DAY

Dr. Corbin and Nicky tarry at the window watching the pair depart. Nicky warily studies his master.

> DR. CORBIN
> See what you can find out about him. I've a hunch he's a runaway. We could use the reward if there is one. Take him with you to O'Meara's tomorrow. She'll know where to find the Ratcatcher.

Nicky's concern melts as he LAUGHS along with his master.

INT. O'MEARA'S HERBAL SHOP - DAY

Nicky enters into the darkened shop with Peter tagging close behind.

>   NICKY
>   Hello, Mother O'Meara are
>   you to home?

>   MOTHER O'MEARA
>   Aye, and who be it who asks?

Peter's vision adjusts to the dimness.
He sees a large figure seated in the
center of the gloom.

>   NICKY
>   'Tis Nicky, Dr. Cobin's
>   servant. I'm here for some
>   hempseed.

>   MOTHER O'MEARA
>   Aye. And who be with ye?

>   NICKY
>   (he pushes Peter
>   forward)
>   This is Peter, he'll be
>   coming in my stead in the
>   future.

Peter looks down at floor and shifts
his weight from foot to foot.

>   MOTHER O'MEARA
>   No cause to be nervous,
>   young Peter. I won't bite
>   you.

Peter startles as a black cat passes
back and forth between his legs. She
CACKLES.

>   MOTHER O'MEARA
>   (CONT'D)
>   Come, Nicky, let's see to
>   your order.

She leads Nicky to the back of the shop. As the two hold a whispered council, Peter looks around. Strings of garlic hang from the ceiling above a counter, upon which a mortar and pestle sit among stacks of pots.

As he lifts the pestle from the mortar, Nicky, now by the door, calls him.

> NICKY
> Time to go.

EXT. O'MEARA'S HERBAL SHOP - DAY

Nicky and Peter depart the shop with Peter carrying their purchase.

> NICKY
> What say you we wander down by the river?

INT. THAMES WAREHOUSE - DAY

Ten MEN throng a small cleared area among stacks of boxes on all sides. Abram, just arrived, pumps the arm of the leader, HEZEKIAH.

> ABRAM
> (He points to an object)
> It this it?

> HEZEKIAH
> Aye. The work of a master craftsman.

                        ABRAM
          Do you think he'll like it?
          I mean, you don't think
          he'll refuse it, do you?

                      HEZEKIAH
          No... I don't think so...

A MAN leads a blindfolded George into
their midst.

                       GEORGE
          I sense others present? Am I
          permitted to remove the
          blindfold yet?

George gropes about him and his hands
alight on Abram's face. The group
LAUGHS.

                  GEORGE (CONT'D)
          Abram Dumbleton, I'd know
          that face anywhere.

They LAUGH again. And Abram reaches up
and removes the blindfold.

Simultaneously the band of men step
away from a portable pulpit revealing
it to George.

                  GEORGE (CONT'D)
          Heaven be praised! A
          portable pulpit. So that is
          what this was all about.

He walks around to the back and steps
up onto it. He stamps his foot on the
surface and it resounds with a solid
THUMP.

Hezekiah beams a smile at Abram.

                    GEORGE (CONT'D)
Gentlemen, I am touched.
Touched to the bottom of my
being, and I thank you. I
thank you for your
confidence in me and for
your decision to stand by me
in my struggles for the
Gospel.

                    ABRAM
Shall we put her to use?

                    GEORGE
Aye, let us find a lighter
and take her to Southwark.

EXT. THAMES QUAY - DAY

Peter mopes along, while Nicky doesn't
seem to have a care.

                    PETER
Shouldn't we be getting
back?

                    NICKY
What's your hurry?

                    PETER
Doesn't Dr. Corbin need
these?

They arrive at...

BLACKFRIARS' STAIRS

                    NICKY
We'll be back long before he
                    (MORE)

                              NICKY (CONT'D)
         does. Wait here. I think I
         see someone I know.

Peter plops down onto the stairs which
run down into the river. He takes out
a sheet of paper and a pencil, unfolds
the paper and starts to draw.

TOP OF BLACKFRIARS' STAIRS

Nicky confers with two men. He talks
respectfully with GREGORY, an older
mysterious figure.

                         GREGORY
         Well, seeing you're here, it
         must mean that the good
         doctor has someone else to
         turn in, eh?

                         NICKY
         Aye, we suspect we've got a
         runaway apprentice. His name
         is Peter Micklewhite. But he
         likes to be called Peter
         Morgan.

He hooks a thumb in Peter's direction.
Sean, standing next to Gregory,
follows the gesture.

                         SEAN
         I seen him before, with
         Roger Morgan.

                         GREGORY
         Well, well, I make it a
         point to do all I can "to"
         the friends of Roger Morgan.

Sean rubs his hands together in anticipation.

                    GREGORY (CONT'D)
          Just don't stand there, go
          find us the grieving master.

Sean jumps at his command and scurries away. Nicky bows to Gregory and is about to return to Peter.

                    GREGORY (CONT'D)
          Stay with me and watch the
          "royal" send-off I've
          planned for William Davis.
               (he glories in Nicky's
                surprise)
          Yes, your master's most
          recent fool.

C.U. PETER'S NEW DRAWING

A grinning skull gapes up from the paper.

                    GEORGE (O.S.)
          You seem a little young to
          be dwelling on death.

PETER

looks up and sees George.

                    PETER
          Yes, sir.

George looks out over the river.

                    GEORGE
          Such a glorious view! A much
               (MORE)

                    GEORGE (CONT'D)
          more fitting subject for
          art, I would think
                (Pauses)
          My name is George--

                    PETER
          --You're Mr. Whitefield,
          aren't you?

                    GEORGE
          Yes, that's right. And you?

                    PETER
          My name is Peter... Peter
          Morgan.

Peter returns to his drawing,
sketching in a post below the skull.
George watches with interest.

                    GEORGE
          Tell me, Peter, where do you
          think you go after you die?

                    PETER
                (Hesitates)
          To heaven... I hope.

                    GEORGE
          Just hope? Wouldn't you like
          to know for certain?

Peter doesn't look up, but he is
listening.

                    GEORGE (CONT'D)
          I find that when people
          "hope" that there is a
          heaven, the also "hope"
          there is no hell.

PETER
Is there really a hell?

GEORGE
I tell you the truth, Peter,
there is. People account me
their enemy because I tell
them the truth, but I can't
help that, God is very plain
on that score. And I also
tell them that Jesus is the
sinner's friend.

They both turn at the breakout of a
commotion above...

TOP OF BLACKFRIAR'S STAIRS

A cloud of PEOPLE buzz around a string
of PRISONERS in chains, escorted by
GUARDS, commanded by an OFFICER. From
all quarters TAUNTS and clods of dirt
zing in at the prisoners. The
prisoners trudge silently on.

Gregory watches with interest and
approval. Most of the missiles find a
tall man, WILLIAM DAVIS, for their
target. Davis looks back at Gregory,
who smiles in reply.

George interposes himself between the
prisoners and their tormentors.

GEORGE
For the love of God, forbear
your cruelty!

The name of "Whitefield" passes as a
MURMUR amongst the prisoners. The
missiles cease, and many in the crowd

look away.

GREGORY'S P.O.V.

George walks up to Davis, takes out a handkerchief and wipes the filth from his face.

C.U. GREGORY

He's not happy.

GEORGE

whispers into the officer's ear. The officer nods in turn, and calls out some orders to the rest of his guards. They halt the prisoners on the stairs, and George takes up a place at their head.

> GEORGE
> I am sure many of you dread the sentence of transportation about to be visited upon you. To some 'twill be like marching into hell itself. Be pleased to believe me when I tell you that America is not hell, 'tis rugged in places, but definitely not a place of torment. And there is a possibility of return from there...
> Not so from the real Hell. No one will be returning from that place. So, this day I would ask you
> (MORE)

                    GEORGE (CONT'D)
to consider. What has the
world, the flesh and the
devil driven you to?
They made promises, promises
of fulfillment that you took
up. They deceived you, and
they circle you now to
accuse and gloat over your
fall.
Not so, with your Heavenly
Father! He loves you, even
though you turned away from
Him and have gone your own
way. Return to Him now and
trust in Him with all of
your heart for He will see
you through.
Let us pray.

Everyone stands in silence.

                    GEORGE (CONT'D)
Lord, I pray for these men
now, that they would extend
forth their hands in faith
to You and take up the cup
of salvation that you freely
offer. For you truly desire
that none should perish.

Every face in the crowd bears the
imprint of George's words, from the
farthest in the back right up to Peter
at George's feet.

LATER

George and Peter watch in silence as
the oars of the boat play in unison
propelling the prisoners down river.

                    PETER
          I wish my father, Roger,
          were with them. Instead
          of...

                    GEORGE
          Instead of what?

                    PETER
               (Looking up at George)
          Sitting in Newgate Prison,
          condemned to the gallows.
          Sir, I'm afraid for my
          father, afraid he stands in
          danger of hell. Would
          you...could you go and speak
          with him?

                    GEORGE
          Most willingly, Peter. I
          shall go this very evening.

Abram joins them. He looks at Peter,
recognition flickers but he can't
place him.

                    ABRAM
               (To George)
          Pulpit's loaded, sir. We can
          leave for Southwark, right
          away.

                    GEORGE
               (He winks at Peter)
          O, to be able to part the
          Thames and walk across on
          dry ground.
               (He shakes Peter's hand)
          'Til we meet again.

THAMES QUAY

A BOATMAN strains at his oars as his craft glides across the river. George waves to Peter and shouts across the water.

>   GEORGE
>   I won't forget your father!

C.U. PETER

Peter's lips compress into a line and he bites them. He makes a decision, cupping his hands around his mouth.

>   PETER
>   Mr. Whitefield, I want you
>   to know... Roger's not
>   really my father...
>   (To himself)
>   I just wanted him to be...

George rises in the sternsheets and calls back to Peter.

>   GEORGE
>   I..will..still..visit..him..
>   .

INT. NEWGATE PRISON/ROGER'S CELL - NIGHT

Roger and Liza sit opposite one another at the table, neither looking at the other. All of a sudden Roger slams the table with his fist. Liza startles out of her daze, and begins to cry. He turns to her.

                    ROGER
                 (Angrily)
        How could he refuse me?

Roger leaps up and kicks the chair
over. Liza cowers.

                    ROGER (CONT'D)
        Now, everyone will!

He looks at Liza, as for the first
time. He softens and holds his arms
out to her. She rushes to him.

They clinch. But over her shoulder his
stare is empty and lost.

INT. THE DAGGER TAVERN - NIGHT

Black, ensconced at a back table all
by himself, prepares to take the first
bite of his meal. The WAITER appears
before him with Sean at his back.

                    SEAN
        Are you the Mr. Black who's
        offering a reward for the
        return of your boy?

Black puts his fork down and motions
Sean to take a seat. As Sean does they
try to size one another up.

                    BLACK
        Aye. And what makes you
        think you have him?

                    SEAN
        We know where he is all
        right. His name is Peter.
             (He indicates Peter's

            height)
About so tall.

                  BLACK
Sounds like him. If it is,
the reward's a pound.

                  SEAN
It'll have to be two.
There's two parties
involved.

                  BLACK
And just who might they be?

                  SEAN
The man I work for is the
Ratcatcher.

The upper hand passes to Sean, a
change comes over Black's features,
respect tinged with fear.

                  BLACK
I...I...I think we can come
to an agreement.

                  SEAN
Good.
    (Rises)
My master will be pleased.

INT. NEWGATE PRISON/ROGER'S CELL -
NIGHT

The prison cleric Purney leans across
the table towards Roger, who has his
back to him.

                    PURNEY
          I will not leave you, Mr.
          Morgan, 'til I have
          discovered the state of your
          soul.

Purney readjusts his demeanor, sitting
back in his chair.

                    PURNEY (CONT'D)
          Come, now, sirrah. Eternity
          awaits, and whatever it has
          in store for you. Surely you
          would not wish to enter in
          to it unconfessed.

Roger, implacable, looks down at his
manacled feet.

                    PURNEY (CONT'D)
          Surely this is no time to
          remain unrepentant. I stand
          ready to assist you in
          making a clean breast of it.
          It's been proved in court
          you have stolen. What else
          weighs on your conscience?
          It is my experience, that it
          all begins slowly, almost
          innocently. Say, the
          breaking of Sabbath one day,
          and that to drink or gamble.

Purney rises from his seat and walks
around to confront Roger, all the time
continuing his harangue.

                    PURNEY (CONT'D)
          What, then, is it, Mr.
          Morgan?
          Swearing? Drunkenness?
          Adultery?

Roger's eyes smolder.

> ROGER
> I have nothing to say to
> you!

> PURNEY
> You reject, then, the mercy
> of the Lord?

> ROGER
> There's the door! Take your
> mercy with you!

Purney whips his hat from the table
and sweeps to the door.

> PURNEY
> No matter. I can fill in the
> details.

Bob enters as Purney leaves. Roger
turns to see who it is.

Bob looks back at the door, then back
to his comrade with his hand to his
nose. He breaks into a laugh and
hobbles to the table.

> BOB
> Purney been dragging you
> over the coals?

Roger, mum, only shrugs his shoulders.

> BOB (CONT'D)
> Well, I've made my peace
> with him. The broadsheet
> should be interesting
> reading. Lord knows I gave
> him enough confessions to
> fill three of them.

>   ROGER
> Exactly why I want nothing
> to do with him. I've seen
> those hawkers at Tyburn,
> selling the story of your
> life before it's ended. All
> about how you went wrong and
> all how you wish you
> hadn't...

>   BOB
> Well, suit yourself, I know
> I am. But just know for
> sure, Ol' Purney's going to
> make up something on his
> own, and you'd been wiser to
> help him along.

Roger gives a cross look, and Bob
quickly changes the topic.

>   BOB (CONT'D)
> Now, I came here to get
> something.

He makes a pretense of looking around.

>   BOB (CONT'D)
> Ah, here 'tis.

He picks up a lace shirt and begins to
change out of the one he has on into
it. He sings a short catch.

>   BOB (CONT'D)
> Gotta look my best for the
> lady.

Roger looks up. Bob notices and takes
the cue.

                    BOB (CONT'D)
Our turnkey approached me
about doing one of the women
prisoners a favor.
For a price that is...
         (He holds up a coin)
Seems she's facing the
noose, too. But if she can
get with child, she can
plead her belly and get off.

Bob finishes buttoning his shirt and
swirls into his coat.

                    BOB (CONT'D)
              (He laughs)
Gotta get enough to pay ol'
Ketch to do the job proper.

With this he pulls his kerchief tight,
fastening it under his adam's apple.

                    BOB (CONT'D)
Come, now, Roger, put a bold
face on it. Live life. Go
out kicking. Want I should
ask if'n she's got a friend?

Roger shakes his head "no."

EXT. NEWGATE STREET - NIGHT

George arrives at the gate to the
prison.

                    GATEKEEPER
Almost closing time, sir.

                    GEORGE
I shan't be long. I want to
visit Roger Morgan.

The gatekeeper turns and motions a
turnkey over.

INT. NEWGATE PRISON/ROGER'S CELL -
NIGHT

George pushes through the door and
into the cell. The candle on the table
flickers and expires in the sudden
gush of air, startling Roger awake.

                    ROGER
          Huh! What! Who's there?

                    GEORGE
          Have no fear, Mr. Morgan.
          It's only a friend of
          Peter's here to visit you.

George takes the candle from the table
and relights it from its companion on
the other side of the room.

                    GEORGE (CONT'D)
          Light! Where would we be
          without light in the world?

                    ROGER
          Light or no light, it
          doesn't change the fact that
          I'm a-sitting here, waiting
          to be hanged.

                    GEORGE
          No. No, that does not change
          the facts. But you must
          admit that if it were not
          for the light, we should not
          know that we were in
          darkness.

>   ROGER
> Oh, that I were o'erta'en by
> darkness already and not
> have to suffer through this
> insufferable waiting.

>   GEORGE
> Sir, you are not longing for
> darkness.

>   ROGER
> What?

>   GEORGE
> Your desire is for something
> better.

>   ROGER
> What? Who are you?

>   GEORGE
> George Whitefield, your
> servant, sir. A friend of
> your friend Peter. He asked
> me to come see you.

Roger sits, his mind in a whirl.

>   ROGER
> I've heard of you. You're
> one o' those Enthusiast
> preachers, aren't you? What?
> Has my Peter turned
> Enthusiast?

>   GEORGE
> Enthusiast. Methodist. Bible
> Moth. All just name calling.
> There is only one name by
> which I want to be called--

                    ROGER
--And what would that be,
sir?

                    GEORGE
May I sit down?
    (Roger nods)
Christian. Simply Christian.

                    ROGER
Listen, if you're like the
Ordinary who was just here,
another one of those carrion
birds, living off a poor
man's misery--

                    GEORGE
I am not here to wrench a
confession out of you. But I
do want to talk to you.
Peter, especially desired me
to do so.

                    ROGER
A fine lad, Peter.

                    GEORGE
A singular lad. And one who
wishes you were his father.

                    ROGER
Aye. That I know for a
truth. But his father I am
not. I'm nobody's father.
And don't care to be either.

                    GEORGE
Ah. But there is One who
cares for you, very deeply.
And desires very much to be
a father to you.

ROGER
Father! What can a father do
for me now? Could he get me
out of here? That's the only
father I'd be interested in.

GEORGE
The Father to whom I refer
is your Heavenly Father, the
One who has given His all
for you.

ROGER
No one's given me a thing.
What I've wanted, I've gone
out and gotten.

GEORGE
What God has for you is far
greater than anything you
have ever gotten for
yourself. But, let me tell
you, sir, what God holds out
to you, you have to reach
out from your side to
accept.

ROGER
What I get, is what I get!
'T's what I deserve, nothing
more, nothing less.

GEORGE
What we deserve, Mr. Morgan,
is death. It's what we've
earned, the wages for our
actions. But God is not
pleased with the death of
any man. His love is
manifest in this, that He
made a way for us to come to
                (MORE)

91

                         GEORGE (CONT'D)
         Him, and that by receiving
         Him, here and now.

Roger stares at the tabletop and
blinks. He reaches for the bottle and
pours himself a large drink.

                         ROGER
         Is this what Peter wanted
         you to talk to me about?

                         GEORGE
         Yes. And more.

Roger throws the drink back and drinks
it in one shot.

                         ROGER
         Listen, I've heard what
         you've had to say, and I
         need some time to think
         about it. I'd like to do
         that on my own.

                         GEORGE
         But today is the day of
         salvation, Mr. Morgan.
         Today, this hour, is the
         time. Surely His Spirit is
         speaking to your heart. Do
         not turn Him away.

Roger rises from his chair and takes a
couple of steps away from the table.

                         ROGER
              (In a low voice)
         You don't understand Mr.
         Whitefield, I've blood on my
         hands.

He turns to George.

> ROGER (CONT'D)
> I killed Peter's father. And
> I'm not sorry one bit that I
> did.

> GEORGE
> Do you think to shock me by
> your revelation? Let me ask
> you - do you know that Moses
> was a murderer? Do you think
> that that would keep him
> from God? Do you think that
> that fact will or could keep
> you from God?

> ROGER
> I don't know what I think. I
> gotta have time to think. I
> gotta have time...

INT. THE SINGING DOVE TAVERN - NIGHT

Full of food and ale, Toomey gives a
full throated rendition of an Irish
tune. Peter listens with delight.

He punctuates the end of the tune with
two hearty TAPS to the table.

This last RATTLES the empty plate in
front of Jerry, who picks up a fork
and tries to dislodge some food from
between his teeth. At last successful,
he casts covetous glances around the
table.

Nicky rises, waves goodbye around the
table and departs.

                    ANDREW
          Every hog his own apple,
          s'what I always say.

Jerry spots an uneaten morsel on
Andrew's plate.

                    JERRY
          Are ya gonna eat that,
          Andrew?

                    PETER
          Do you know any more,
          Toomey?

                    ANDREW
          Yeah, Toomey, how 'bout a
          drinkin' song?

                    JERRY
          Andrew, are you going to
          finish--

                    ANDREW
          A toast, gentlemen. To our
          continued success! And to
          our venture on the road!

                    TOOMEY
          How long'll you be gone?

                    ANDREW
          We'll be back in a week, or
          so. By Tyburn Fair for sure.

Jerry slides his hand across the table
towards Andrew's plate. Liza's arrival
cuts this action short.

                    LIZA
          Jerry, have ya seen Tiny?

Her urgency brings the table to silence.

> JERRY
>
> No, Liza.

She surveys the rest of the table. All shake their heads "no". Fear mounts in Peter.

> LIZA
>
> I've got to talk to the Ratcatcher, and plead for Roger's life.

She turns and walks out. Peter stumbles to his feet, but Andrew grabs him and forcefully holds him back.

> ANDREW
>
> It's no good, Peter! Let it go! There's nothing you can do!

> PETER
>
> Let me go!

He slips under Andrew's arm and runs away. Jerry rises to join him, but a stern look from Andrew causes him to docilely sit back down.

> ANDREW
>
> How about a game of chance?

EXT. A LONDON SQUARE - NIGHT

Peter arrives at the edge of the square and stops. Liza has found Tiny, they stand talking in front of a tavern on the other side.

George walks up behind Peter.

> GEORGE
> And how's my young friend
> Peter?

Peter turns.

> GEORGE (CONT'D)
> Would you like me to
> accompany you home? We could
> talk about your friend
> Roger.

Peter looks back. Liza and Tiny are
still talking.

> GEORGE (CONT'D)
> I just now left your friend.
> We had a nice long talk. He
> sends his respects.

Peter turns back to George.

> PETER
> Did you warn him about hell?

> GEORGE
> Aye, that I did. He needs
> time to think.
> (He pats him
> reassuringly)
> I promise you, lad, I'll pay
> him another visit before the
> day...

Peter spins around to look across the
square. They're gone.

Without a word Peter breaks into a
run.

                    GEORGE (CONT'D)
          Peter! What's wrong?

AROUND THE CORNER

                    PETER
          Mama! Tiny! Wait!

The two stop as he runs up to them.

                    PETER (CONT'D)
          Take me with you!

Liza walks on, on her own, leaving
Tiny to talk to the boy.

                    TINY
               Listen, Peter, neither of
               you should be coming with
               me--

                    PETER
          I don't care, I'm coming!

Peter's fierceness silences Tiny. They
walk after Liza.

EXT. DYOT STREET/RATCATCHER'S CASTLE -
NIGHT

The trio halts across from a once fine
mansion, now dilapidated and
foreboding. They cross over and enter
the complex via a ...

RATCATCHER'S CASTLE/NARROW LANE

Which is hemmed in by hovels. The lane
branches in all directions becoming a

veritable labyrinth. PEOPLE, in rags, watch their passing in silence, but with undisguised interest. It finally debauches onto a...

RATCATCHER'S CASTLE/COURTYARD

> GUARD
> Halt! Who're you?

> TINY
> We're here to see the
> Ratcatcher.

> GUARD
> I didn't ask who you wanted
> to see, I asked who you
> were.

> TINY
> I'm Tiny Cahoon. Don't
> worry, the Ratcatcher will
> see me.

> GUARD
> We'll see about that.

The guard disappears into the woodwork. While he's gone, they look around. Bales of skins are stacked everywhere in the courtyard, and one corner is set up as a tannery.

> GUARD (CONT'D)
> (Returning)
> It's all right, you can go
> in.

Liza and Peter follow Tiny into the inner sanctum.

INT. RATCATCHER'S CASTLE/ THE INNER
SANCTUM

Dozens of candles in its single
chandelier light the panelled room.
Gregory, the Ratcatcher, beckons the
trio forward to admire with him a
tiger pelt mounted on the wall.

> GREGORY
> One of my men found it.
> Magnificent, don't you
> think?

Peter stares with gaping mouth. Liza
pushes forward.

> LIZA
> All I see is a moth-eaten
> rug!

> GREGORY
> (To Tiny)
> Silence your woman, or I'll
> have your head mounted up
> there with it.

Tiny pulls her behind his back.

> TINY
> (Under his breath)
> Shut up, or you'll get us
> killed!

She holds herself in check, defiantly.
Gregory regarding them sullenly,
notices Peter for the first time, and
makes a mental calculation.

> GREGORY
> This is about Roger Morgan
> again, isn't it?
> My original decision stands.

                    LIZA
          We can pay you!

Tiny cuts her off.

                    TINY
          Please, forgive her, sir.
          She is in love with Roger
          and--

                    GREGORY
               (Deigning to talk to
                her)
          Pay me with what?
               (Cuts off her protest)
          There is nothing you have
          that is not by rights mine
          to begin with.

                    TINY
          Surely, if Roger owes you
          anything, it makes more
          sense to have him alive to
          work off the debt.

                    LIZA
          I have my own--

                    GREGORY
          Not enough! Not enough! I am
          king here and disloyalty
          will be punished.

                    PETER
          Please, sir, would you take
          me instead?

                    GREGORY
          Lad, you are mine already.

                    TINY
          But--

                    LIZA
          You can't--

                    GREGORY
          Can't what? Want to call the
          night watchman? I have my
          own night watchman.

Peter makes a run for the door, but
runs into the arms of Sean.

                    GREGORY (CONT'D)
          Behold, my night watchman!
                (to Sean)
          Lock him up!
                (turning to Tiny and
                 Liza)
          Get out of here!

EXT. DR. CORBIN'S HOUSE - DAY

In the gray light before dawn, Dr.
Corbin and Nicky cross the courtyard
to the waiting wagon. Jerry and Andrew
wait up beside the WAGONEER.

                    DR. CORBIN
          Is all ready?

                    WAGONEER
          Aye.

                    JERRY
          Peter isn't here yet.

Corbin looks at Nicky. He shrugs his
shoulders in reply.

                    DR. CORBIN
          We can't wait. Let's go.

EXT. RATCATCHER'S CASTLE/COURTYARD
(THREE DAYS LATER)

A makeshift cage huddles against the
wall of the courtyard. Inside, Peter
slumbers in a nest of rags.

Sean enters the courtyard dragging a
GROWLING dog. Peter stirs at the noise
and sits up when Sean shoves Codger
into the cage with him.

Codger calms down and goes to Peter.
Peter draws him into a hug, burying
his head in his fur. Codger responds
by licking his ear. Sean picks up a
skin from a nearby bale and compares
it to Codger's.

                    SEAN
          Don't get too attached--

Gregory enters from his chamber. Sean
draws his attention to the dog.

                    SEAN (CONT'D)
          Another bit of revenue.

                    GREGORY
          So when's Black paying up?

                    SEAN
          He promises the end of the
          week. Come Tyburn Fair. And
          he knows interest has
          accrued.

EXT. PARISH ROUNDHOUSE (FOUR NIGHTS
LATER)

An INNKEEPER waddles from his inn
across to the roundhouse of the night

watchmen, where Abram enjoys the night
air and his pipe.

> INNKEEPER
> G'd evening, Abram. I've got
> a gentleman who wants to be
> woken at the sixth hour.

His mind on other matters, Abram only
nods.

> INNKEEPER
> Did you hear me Abram?

> ABRAM
> Aye, Toby, I'll wake the
> gentleman and see him on his
> way.

> INNKEEPER
> He's in the first room at
> the top of the stairs. Don't
> forget. He doesn't want to
> be late for Tyburn.

The innkeeper waddles back to the inn.

INT. PARISH ROUNDHOUSE

Abram grabs Jacob's stockinged foot
and jerks him awake.

> ABRAM
> Time to get up, Jacob.

> JACOB
> Hey! Let go of my foot!

> ABRAM
> I said "time to get up."

                    JACOB
          So? I'm excused.

                    ABRAM
          I'll talk to Mr. Feeney
          about this.

Jacob reassumes his "working
position."

                    JACOB
          You'll see him tonight.

EXT. DR. CORBIN'S HOUSE - NIGHT

The wagon rumbles into the courtyard,
its occupants dusty and tired from the
road. Corbin and Nicky dismount and
enter the house. Andrew and Jerry help
the wagoneer unload.

As they back the wagon into the
stable, Jenny appears.

                    JENNY
          Andrew, I'm so glad to see
          you.

Andrew puts down what he's carrying
and rushes to kiss her. Jerry follows.

                    ANDREW
          Absence hath made the heart
          grow fonder.

                    JENNY
               (including Jerry in)
          I need your help. Peter
          needs your help.

                    ANDREW
          Where's Liza? Shouldn't--

                    JENNY
          She's too wrought. Roger,
          you know.

                    JERRY
          What's happened to Peter?

EXT. RATCATCHER'S CASTLE/COURTYARD -
NIGHT

Peter sits in the cage sketching while
Codger naps at his feet. Codger stirs
at the sound of BARKING. A sickening
CRUNCH cuts the barking short. Codger
WHINES. Peter reaches down and pets
him to comfort him.

                    PETER
          It's all right, boy. Our
          Heavenly Father will see us
          through this. Just you wait.

From memory he has almost completed a
sketch of Alice.

EXT. PARISH ROUNDHOUSE - NIGHT

Abram strides forward from the
roundhouse to meet Feeney.

                    ABRAM
          Mr. Feeney, I need to talk
          with you.

Feeney stops and spins around, his
fierce aspect for an instant cows
Abram. But Abram gathers his courage.

                    ABRAM (CONT'D)
          Mr. Feeney, I find that I
          can no longer countenance
          certain things transpiring
          in this parish.

                    FEENEY
          Your meaning, sir?

                    ABRAM
          If you persist in turning a
          blind eye to the unlawful
          practices that are going on
          under our noses, practices
          that you are sworn to stop
          as a parish officer, I shall
          go to the justice of the
          peace.

                    FEENEY
          Practices? What practices?

                    ABRAM
          You know very well what
          practices.

Feeney turns on his heel and stalks
away, shouting back:

                    FEENEY
          You are relieved, sirrah.

INT. NEWGATE PRISON/CHAPEL - NIGHT

Pandemonium reigns. All the condemned
PRISONERS are drunk, most of them
drunk on their butts. The few still on
their feet chase one another around
the chapel, SCREAMING.

Purney stands at the back of a closed

coffin, which substitutes for his
lectern.

                    PURNEY
          Order!!

Roger sits, back to the wall, on the
bare floor, all feeling anesthetized.

                    PURNEY (CONT'D)
          Order, I say!

Bob, chasing another prisoner, catches
him and snatches a bottle from him.
The other prisoner falls down in a
heap, LAUGHING hysterically. Holding
the bottle, Bob upends it, revealing
it to be empty.

                    PURNEY (CONT'D)
          You are in the house of God!

At this, the noise level drops a tiny
bit, and encouraged, Purney starts his
sermon.

                    PURNEY (CONT'D)
          In a short while you will
          hear the bellman toll the
          hour. 'Twill announce the
          last day of your lives--

A fight breaks out between two
prisoners across from Roger. Bob wades
through the room and rescues a bottle,
this time full. Seeing Roger, Bob
plops down beside him.

The fight continues, gathering to
itself other prisoners loud in their
bets on the outcome. Purney,
exasperated, throws his hands in the

air.

>   PURNEY (CONT'D)
>   I wash my hands of you.

A ragged CHEER spreads around the
chapel. Bob uncorks the bottle with
his teeth and offers the first swig to
Roger. Roger takes a pull and passes
it back. After taking a swig himself,
Bob points with the bottle at his
shoes.

C.U. BOB'S SHOES

Silver shoe buckles sparkle.

>   BOB (O.S.)
>   My passport to a quick
>   death.

Roger looks puzzled.

>   BOB (CONT'D)
>   Part o' my deal with Ketch.
>   I give him this coin...
>   (He takes out a guinea)
>   And when I'm dead he takes
>   these too.

>   ROGER
>   I'm not givin' the blood-
>   sucker a blessed thing.

Bob shakes his head.

>   BOB
>   Roger, you don't know when
>   it's your own best interests
>   to play the game.

EXT. ABRAM'S HOUSE - NIGHT

Abram returns from work, just as
George arrives at his door.

>   GEORGE
>   They told me I would find
>   you home.
>
>   ABRAM
>   Aye, it's done. And I feel a
>   great weight lifted.
>
>   GEORGE
>   Abram, I am here to ask a
>   favor of you.
>   (pauses)
>   I've doubly committed myself
>   for tomorrow and I was
>   wondering--
>
>   ABRAM
>   As long as it's not standing
>   up in front preaching--
>
>   GEORGE
>   There's a prisoner condemned
>   to die, a close friend of
>   the lad we met down by the
>   river a while ago.
>
>   ABRAM
>   But, George, I wouldn't know
>   what to say--
>
>   GEORGE
>   All you need do, my friend,
>   is sit with him and share
>   the Scriptures, you know
>   them well enough. God will
>   take care of the rest.
>   (Abram is still

           hesitant)
     Show the love of Jesus to a
     man about to die.

              ABRAM
     All right, I will. How will
     I know him?

EXT. NEWGATE PRISON - DAY

Roger idles by his cart. Two CARTMEN
wrestle with a wheel to put it back on
the cart's axle. The rest of the
PRISONERS, sit in their carts next to
their coffins.

The SHERIFF on his horse tramps
impatiently back and forth at the head
of the procession. His LIEUTENANT
joins him.

             SHERIFF
     If they can't fix it, tell
     them to get another!

MOMENTS LATER

Roger, now in the cart, grabs the rail
to keep his balance as it lurches
forward to join the procession. Bob,
whose cart precedes his, raises his
hand in salute, then turns to face
forward. Bob takes his coin from his
pocket to reassure himself of its
presence. Satisfied, he returns it to
its place.

ST. SEPULCHRE'S CHURCH NEAR NEWGATE
PRISON

Abram stops one of the mounted GUARDS
and after a brief interchange, the
guard points in an exaggerated fashion
to the far end of the column.

As each cart passes in front of the
church a group of WOMEN give each
prisoner a nosegay. Abram passes them
as they present Bob with his.

Abram steps up to the guard by Roger's
cart, and after another short
conversation is allowed to mount
into...

ROGER'S CART

Roger moves from the center and leans
against the side rail.

> ABRAM
> Roger Morgan?

> ROGER
> Aye?

> ABRAM
> My name is Abram, and I'm
> here on the behalf of Mr.
> Whitefield.

Roger motions for Abram to take the
opposite rail. Just as he takes this
position the cart stops in front of
the group of women. One of them
presents the last bouquet to Abram.

>   WOMAN
>   The peace of the Lord be
>   with you.

Roger chuckles, and Abram joins in.
The cart jolts forward again. Abram
passes the bouquet to Roger.

>   ABRAM
>   Truly, I do wish you the
>   peace of God.

Roger nods, holds the bouquet to his
nose and smells it.

>   ROGER
>   One last breath of spring...

He reaches forward and places it on
the coffin.

>   ABRAM
>   Have you made your peace
>   with God, Mr. Morgan?

>   ROGER
>   You can call me by my
>   Christian name.

Roger's face clouds over.

>   ABRAM
>   Can you tell me what
>   troubles you, Roger?

>   ROGER
>   I feel so far away from
>   God...and worse I feel a
>   very hypocrite to even think
>   about turning to him now at
>   this point...after all I've
>   done.

> ABRAM
> That's the enemy of your
> soul talking. Not the Lord.

> ROGER
> What do I do?

> ABRAM
> Repent and believe. Forsake
> your way and go His.

Roger hangs his head.

> ROGER
> The only place I'm going now
> is the gallows. It's too
> late for me to do anything
> that could offset my sin.

> ABRAM
> But don't you understand,
> Roger, that no one can do
> anything to offset their
> sins, for Scripture says
> that good works, in
> themselves cannot save us.
> Only faith in Jesus Christ
> can save us. We are
> justified by faith.

> ROGER
> What does that mean?

> ABRAM
> Let me tell you a story. St.
> Luke in his gospel tells
> about two men who were
> crucified at the same time
> as our Lord. One reviled the
> Lord and cursed Him. But the
> other, a man who probably
> (MORE)

                    ABRAM (CONT'D)
felt much the same as
yourself, saw something in
Jesus that you should see...

                    ROGER
What's that?

                    ABRAM
His Lordship. It's something
I've learned. God is so much
bigger than any of us, than
any of our problems. He's
really much closer to you
than you know. That man who
saw His Lordship, simply
asked Jesus to remember him.
And Jesus replied to him,
"Today thou shalt be with me
in paradise."

                    ROGER
But..but, how could He let
him in...?

                    ABRAM
You think that God cannot
pardon sin justly? But I
tell you that God's law was
upheld. Jesus took the due
punishment for all
lawbreakers.

                    ROGER
But, Abram, you don't
know...

                    ABRAM
'Tis it you think you've
committed the most horrible,
the most unforgivable sin?

Roger's look betrays his assent to

this truth.

> ABRAM (CONT'D)
> Let's look at it in another
> way. If one commits even a
> minor sin, say lying,
> Scripture says that it's the
> same as murder for they are
> against His law and to break
> one is the same as breaking
> all.

> ROGER
> Then, there be none
> innocent.

> ABRAM
> Exactly. And to come back to
> the point of the story of
> the thief on the cross, he
> saw that Jesus could do that
> which he could not do
> himself. He could and did
> forgive his sin. Scripture
> is full of the promises of
> God, chief of which is the
> promise of eternal life to
> them who believe in His
> name. That thief believed
> and trusted that Jesus was
> Lord. He reached out and
> accepted that gift which was
> offered.

> ROGER
> I think I remember Mr.
> Whitefield saying something
> similar.

> ABRAM
> The messengers may differ
>   (MORE)

                    ABRAM (CONT'D)
but the message, if they're
true messengers will be the
same. For the message is not
their own, it is the Word of
God. And as with any word
you have to decide if you're
going to trust it or not.
Are you, Roger, are you
going to trust His promise
to you?

                    ROGER
Aye. But, Abram, could you
help me? I don't know how.

Abram kneels to pray and Roger kneels
beside him.

HOLBORN, THE GEORGE INN - LATER

Throngs of PEOPLE fill both sides of
the street allowing just room enough
for the mounted officials and the
prisoners in their carts to pass
along. The sheriff signals a halt to
the procession in front of the Inn.
Roger in the last cart is now alone.

Liza presses through the crowd
surrounding Roger, carrying a pitcher
of ale. She talks in the ear of the
guard who then allows her to pass.
Roger sees her, reaches down for her
hand and pulls her up into the cart.

                    LIZA
Roger!
        (She hugs him)
My love, my love!

She clings to his tall frame, burying
her face in his chest to hide her
tears. He throws his arms protectively
around her.

>ROGER
>There now, be brave, my
>pretty. Let me remember your
>beauty...

He brushes her tears tenderly away
with his thumbs, and chucks her under
the chin lifting her lips to his.

>LIZA
>You know... I won't--

>ROGER
>--I know...and I don't
>expect you to be there. Let
>this be our goodbye.

He kisses her again. As they part
surprise registers on her face.
Something is different. He bends to
her and whispers in her ear.

BOB

from his exalted position on his cart,
glows with animal spirits at his
FRIENDS all around him. He lifts a
giant tankard.

>BOB
>To the good life!

>A FRIEND
>Aye! To life!

The others chime in, in a RAUCOUS
CHORUS. Bob upends the tankard and

chugs the ale in a single swallow,
twin rivulets overflowing down both
sides of his face. He flings the
tankard into the crowd. His friends
CHEER.

Tiny looks on with professional
interest.

> A FRIEND (CONT'D)
> Three cheers for Bob
> Trinkett!

> OTHER FRIENDS
> Huzza! HUZza! HUZZA!

The FRIEND hands him another tankard.
Bob takes it with a grin and steps
back with unsteady feet. He falls on
his backside, drenching himself with
the ale. Some friends spring up into
the cart to help him to his feet, Tiny
among them.

> GUARD
> Here! We'll have none o'
> that. Unhand him and get out
> of the cart!

They stand Bob to his feet, then
reluctantly debark. Tiny brushes
against Bob as he climbs out. The
guard brandishes his bayonet at them.

> GUARD (CONT'D)
> Come on! Be quick about it!

Bob reaches down and takes a friend's
tankard.

> BOB
> To your health!

> (Aside to the guard)
> Ya louse!

The guard only glares.

The sheriff holds his watch in his hand. He beckons to his lieutenant.

> SHERIFF
> Pass the word to move on. And have the guards move that rabble back.

Tiny holds the gold piece up before his face, then returns it to his pocket. Looking behind him he sees Roger in his cart. He begins to move towards him, but stops, hesitates, hangs his head and walks away.

Roger bends over the rail and hands the empty tankard to a WELL-WISHER.

> ROGER
> Right refreshing, my lad!

> WELL-WISHER
> Do ye want some more?

Roger shakes his head "no," looking Liza in the eyes. The command of the sheriff arrives and the guards move everyone back from the carts.

ROGER'S P.O.V.

The cart begins to move forward. The crowd forms itself behind his cart, cutting off his view of Liza.

EXT. RATCATCHER'S CASTLE/COURTYARD - DAY

Sean shakes Peter's cage.

> SEAN
> Time to rejoin your lord and master!

> PETER
> Mr. Black may be my master but he's not my lord.

> SEAN
> So be it! Say goodbye to the dog.

AROUND THE CORNER

Andrew pulls his head back to talk with Jerry.

> ANDREW
> There's only two. Get ready.

BACK TO SCENE

Sean has just opened the cage to extract Peter, when the guard raises an alarm. He looks behind him.

SEAN'S P.O.V.

A twelve foot giant in a flowing cape lumbers around the corner and comes straight for them.

BACK TO SCENE

The guard makes for him, cudgel swinging. Andrew, standing on Jerry's shoulders, flings the cape into the air over the charging guard, and springs off of his friend into a somersault that lands square on Sean.

As Jerry trusses the guard in the entangling cape, Andrew leans over Sean's limp form and binds his hands.

>   JERRY
>   Ho Peter. Things looking up?

Peter runs to his waiting arms and a happy Codger wags up beside them.

Andrew shoves Sean into the cage and locks the door.

Sean, face down in the filthy rags, flips over to his back and looks up at Andrew.

>   ANDREW
>   How's it feel?

>   SEAN
>   The last thing you'll ever
>   feel is my knife when I draw
>   it out of your heart!

>   ANDREW
>   Enough! You're scaring me.
>   (to Peter and Jerry)
>   Come on, gentlemen.

>   SEAN
>   You'll curse the day you
>   were born! I'll find you.

EXT. DYOT STREET - DAY

The trio plus Codger exit from the Ratcatcher's Castle at a run. The procession to Tyburn blocks the cross street ahead. Roger's cart passes in view.

> PETER
>> Roger!

Andrew grabs his arm, but he shakes it loose.

> ANDREW
> Don't be a fool, Peter. There's nothing you can do!

> PETER
> You'll help me, won't you, Jerry?

He sadly shakes his head.

> JERRY
> I'm sorry, lad. I'm a wanted man. I can't show my face there.

> PETER
>> Well, I'm going.

He takes off with Codger at his heels.

OXFORD STREET

The street flows like a river in flood, but in this case choked with people buoyed by a boisterous holiday spirit.

Codger stops in his tracks and WHINES.

                    PETER
          Come on, boy.

Codger has other ideas, he takes off
running in the opposite direction.
Peter turns his attention to the last
of the procession, the SPEARMEN,
arriving at Tyburn, about a mile away.
He wavers a second, then plunges in,
his panic growing.

TYBURN

A pigeon appears over the crowd, let
loose to announce the approach of the
carts. Expectant SHOUTS of "They're
Here!" and "the Carts" bubble up from
the crowd.

The Sheriff, stern and dignified,
parts the crowd. Purney's coach
follows, then the condemned men's
carts.

The spearmen bring up the rear, their
weapons flashing in the sunlight.

                    PHILLIP-IN-THE-TUB
          Read their confessions! Only
          a ha'penny each.

Mr. Black and Gregory perch next to
him.

                    BLACK
          When's your man going to get
          here?

                    GREGORY
          Don't worry, you can count
          on Sean to have your brat
          here for you. Now that
          you've paid.

                    GEORGE (O.S.)
          The call of God calls us
          away from this unthinking,
          this careless world. We must
          die unto ourselves that we
          may live unto Him.

INT. LADY HASTINGS' SALON - SAME TIME

LADY HASTINGS looks around at her
fellow ARISTOCRATS to see the effect
of George's preaching upon them. Every
eye is glued upon him.

Concern plays across the brow of her
neighbor, as with each word the
furrows deepen.

                    GEORGE
          For if one persists in
          heeding the call of this
          world, you shall be caught
          up in its ways, in its
          wisdom. And the fruit you
          thought to reap will turn to
          ashes with the realization
          that the piper calling the
          tune was the very enemy of
          your soul. You were trapped
          in the snare, seduced there
          by your own desires.

BACK TO THE SCENE AT TYBURN

Ketch, more than a little drunk,
stumbles over to Bob's cart, now at
rest under a cross-beam of the
gallows. He mounts the back of the
cart and places a noose over Bob's
head.

> KETCH
> (whispers)
> Which pocket is she in?

Bob looks down to the right. Ketch
slips his hand in and comes up empty.

> BOB
> Whadda ya know, I've been
> robbed.

Ketch, unamused, wrenches the knot
around to the front and pushes it home
to his throat.

> KETCH
> No, you've cheated yerself.

Bob, left standing in the cart, sobers
quickly under the watchful eyes of the
crowd. Ketch whips the cart's horse to
get it moving.

As the cart moves forward, Bob panics.
He tries to step up onto the rail of
the cart, to end his life quickly, but
trips and stumbles backward, his feet
dragging on the tail of the cart
before it slips away from beneath him.
Bob's body writhes at the end of the
rope.

A few of Bob's friends run out from
the crowd and tackle his feet, pulling

him down, hoping to end his agony.

> GEORGE (O.S.)
> It is appointed to a man
> once to die. And then the
> judgment...

Peter arrives at the back of the
throng and dives in to force his way
to the front of the crush of people.
He comes to rest by Phillip-in-the-
Tub.

PETER'S P.O.V.

Fifteen bodies hang from the gallows.
One man, yet remains in his cart.
Roger submits his head to the noose,
and looks skyward.

> GEORGE (V.O.)
> Our Lord Jesus submitted to
> death. He took the judgment
> due each one of us.

GREGORY

Spots Peter and furtively steps away
from Black to stand behind him.

> GEORGE (V.O.)
> He who knew no sin became
> sin for us, bearing the full
> penalty...

PHILIP-IN-THE-TUB

receives a coin and gives a broadsheet
in exchange.

                                    GEORGE (V.O.)
                         ...in exchange for our sin
                         He gave us His
                         righteousness. So as to
                         judgment we are acquitted...

PETER

struggles to control his lower lip,
unable to take his eyes from the
scene. Roger's body falls with a jerk
and is still.

                                    GEORGE (V.O.)
                         Therefore, death for the
                         Christian holds no terror.
                         What the world views as
                         defeat, we view as victory.

ON THE GALLOWS

all sixteen bodies hang in the silence
of death.

PETER

draws the back of his hand across his
eyes to wipe the tears away.

                                    GEORGE (V.O.)
                         The victory that the Lord
                         won, He shares with us.

Peter turns to walk away, only to be
greeted by the waiting clutches of the
Ratcatcher.

                              GREGORY
          I don't know how you got
          here, but I thank my lucky
          star you did.

He hands him over to Black. Peter is
too numb to care.

INT. THE BISHOP'S PALACE - DAY (ONE
WEEK LATER)

The quill in the Gibson's hand moves
like a live creature, leaving a
continuous track across the page.
Feeney enters and crosses to the
writing table. The bishop holds up a
hand until he finishes the line with a
flourish. He throws the quill down and
looks up to Feeney.

                              GIBSON
          Well?

                              FEENEY
          Yesterday's post, sir.

He hands the bishop a stack of
letters. He turns to leave.

                              GIBSON
          I have a matter for you to
          attend to.

The bishop picks up a packet and hands
it to him.

                              GIBSON (CONT'D)
          I want you to deliver this
          to Mr. Whitefield. It's a
          subscription that I promised
          to give him for his
                    (MORE)

                    GIBSON (CONT'D)
orphanage...in a moment of
weakness.

                    FEENEY
Very well, sir. I am going
down to the city, I shall
endeavor to deliver it.

He slips it into his coat pocket.

                    GIBSON
You needn't go so far. I
hear he will be at
Moorfields today.

INT. BLACK'S HOUSE - DAY

Peter listlessly rebuilds the fire on
the hearth. He glances up at his
chains hanging from their peg on the
wall. A KNOCK sounds at the front
door. Black seated at the table rises
and crosses to open it.

Feeney enters. He sees Peter and
smirks.

                    FEENEY
Think you can hold him this
time?

                    BLACK
        (To Peter)
Fetch us some beer.
        (to Feeney)
I've got him this time. For
good.

                              FEENEY
                    Well, you know, I can always
                    find more foundlings for
                    you.

AT THE TABLE

Feeney takes a packet out of his
pocket and passes it to Black.

                              FEENEY
                    I can get you more, but try
                    to keep the price down.

                              BLACK
                    Don't worry. Sean, who works
                    for the Ratcatcher, has
                    someone who'll do it for
                    next to nothing.

Feeney and Black laugh. Peter
shudders. He steps up to pour the
beer.

                              BLACK (CONT'D)
                    All we need to know is where
                    and when to do it.

                              FEENEY
                    I've learned that Whitefield
                    will be at Moorfields today.

This grabs Peter's attention. He
finishes pouring and retreats from the
table but not out of ear shot.

                              BLACK
                    Sounds like the perfect
                    place to silence that
                    meddler.

Black grows thoughtful and turns around to look at Peter. He rises from the table and takes down Peter's chains, and motions him over.

> BLACK (CONT'D)
> Today may be a holiday for most apprentices. But not for you.

Peter takes one look at him and breaks for the door. Feeney cuts him off. Peter reverses direction and ducks under Black's lunge, who instead collides with Feeney.

Peter stops to catch his breath and wits by the fireplace. In a split second he decides. He kicks a pot of water onto the fire and swings out a kettle resting on its hook. Securing a cloth around his hands, he dives into the steam, now billowing into the room and goes up the chimney. Black is in time to catch his ankle, but Peter kicks himself free. The ROARING from the thwarted men fills the chimney.

EXT. BLACK'S ROOF - DAY

Peter's shadow emerges from the mixture of smoke and steam, startling a pair of cats. They skitter down the back slope of the roof, raising a CLATTER.

> FEENEY (O.S.)
> He's going down the back side.

As he hears the CLICK of their shoes in the back courtyard, Peter jumps to the next roof, and continues on for two more before reaching a window he can access.

EXT. MOORFIELDS - DAY

Peter arrives at Moorfields to find it set up for every kind of entertainment and every kind of vendor. He passes PUPPETEERS, SNAKE HANDLERS, DWARVES, and a BEARDED LADY. The GINGERBREAD MAN pushes his wares, the GIN SELLERS vie among one another, and, yes, the MOUNTEBANKS loudly hawk their cures. He recognizes Dr. Corbin's stage, but presses on, for across the field he sees George's portable pulpit with by far the largest crowd in front of it.

With a flourish, George mounts his pulpit. He moves to the front rail and throws his arms out to the crowd.

                    GEORGE
               (His voice booming)
          Welcome, my friends,
          welcome.

DR. CORBIN'S BOOTH

Andrew looks up from putting his make up on, he can clearly hear George's voice. He walks around to the front of the booth. George is a speck in the distance. Dr. Corbin joins him to look at George's burgeoning crowd.

                    GEORGE
          My text for today is taken
                    (MORE)

132

                    GEORGE (CONT'D)
from Numbers 21, "And Moses
said, 'If you look on the
raised serpent and believe,
ye shall be healed.'" Now we
know that God's Word is
given to us for an example.

Jenny and Tiny cross Peter's path.
They call out to him, but he is intent
on his destination.

                    GEORGE (O.S.)
                    (CONT'D)
It is replete with lessons
of how to live and how not
to live. Oh, how the
Israelites needed to learn
how to live! How we all need
to know how we should live!
And not just merely existing
but life that is truly life,
abundant and overflowing.

Peter skirts the edge of the crowd
before finding a gap and plunges in.

                    GEORGE (CONT'D)
Now, as you know, the
Israelites were God's
children, His chosen ones,
selected from all who lived
on the face of the earth. In
Exodus we are told that
God's people had fallen on
hard times, they were made
slaves to the slaves in the
land of Egypt. And their
service was hard, and they
were sore pressed. So
pressed that they cried out
to the Lord their God. And
                    (MORE)

                    GEORGE (CONT'D)
God heard their cries for
help. He heard and sent His
servant Moses, a humble man,
the most humble of his day.
At God's command he
performed many a wonder that
struck awe in the sorcerers
of pharaoh - the power of
darkness could not prevail
against the light. With a
mighty uplifted right hand
the Lord delivered His
people out of the land of
Egypt.

Tiny likes what he sees and dispatches
Jenny into the midst of the multitude.

                    GEORGE (O.S.)
                    (CONT'D)
But that was only the
beginning of the wonders
that God had in store for
His own. Trapped by the sea
with Pharaoh and his
chariots coming to crush
them, they looked to Moses,
who sought God for help
again. And God instructed
him to raise his rod and
command the waters to part.
And they did, they rose up
to great walls of water on
both sides, and the
multitude crossed over on
dry land.

Peter finally reaches the front and
scans the faces of the people at hand.
George notices and nods to him.

                    GEORGE (CONT'D)
Imagine, if you will,
needing to get to Southwark
and there were no London
Bridge, no boats to be had.
Only you standing on the
quay, with death staring you
in the face, and breathing
down your neck. You cry out
to God in your distress. And
He answers. The Thames stops
flowing, and piles the
waters up as high as St.
Paul's. And as if that were
not enough, he dries the mud
of the river bottom that you
may cross over dry shod.

Jenny ranges here and there but can't
help listening too.

                    GEORGE (CONT'D)
Once safe on the other
shore, with Death defeated
behind you, do you kneel
down and thank the One who
saved you? Do you remember
Him with gratitude? Yes,
perhaps,...for the moment.
You'll proclaim a festival,
even a solemn feast. But
what about the next day, the
next problem, the next need?
Are we indeed any better
than the Israelites? How
soon after did they forget
their wonder-working God? A
year? A month? A day? Moses,
why did you bring us into
this desert to die? We have
no food, no drink. We forget
so soon. Moses asks God, God
                    (MORE)

                         GEORGE (CONT'D)
gives food - from the very
Heaven. God gives drink -
gushing from a rock. God
knows how to provide for His
people. He is faithful...but
are we? God delivers us from
an affliction, but what
happens then? We fall into
another. It happened to the
Israelites. God delivered
them from their enemies from
Arad. But then only to face
the problem again - nothing
to eat or drink. Did they
stop and think, we've been
this way before, we have
gone from triumph to
triumph. No, they succumb to
a dire temptation, they sink
back into the pit from which
they had been rescued.

DR. CORBIN'S BOOTH

No one stands outside.

                         GEORGE (O.S.)
Stop...Listen...do you here
it? We are outside their
camp. There from that tent.
Did you hear it? Murmur. And
from that one?

INT. DR. CORBIN'S BOOTH

The mountebank and his crew talk MOS.

                    GEORGE (O.S.)
Murmur, murmur. What is it
you say? Surely nothing
we've heard before. Why we
cannot even make out what it
is they are saying? They are
complaining against God.
What you say? We have never
been so bold. Now, really.
Never?

BACK TO GEORGE

                    GEORGE
Ah, you say, the Israelites
made it their practice. You
shy away from your own
culpability. Fine, for the
moment. Let's look at the
Israelites here. Let's hold
up the mirror of God's Word,
then we shall see ourselves.
Aye, they did murmur against
God. And murmur and murmur,
they who had seen the great
deliverances, they who had
repeatedly benefited from
the mercies and kindnesses
of God. They complained
against their Judge. And
brought on their undoing.

SEAN AND EGBERT

arrive together. Their target George
is easy to see. They smile at one
another. They split up to reconnoiter.

                    GEORGE (O.S.)
Serpents with the sting of
death were let loose among
them, striking right and
left with unrelenting
ferocity, decimating their
number. Great then were the
cries unto God. Dire
necessity spoke. And what
then, was God's response? He
provided a way of healing.
But He so arranged it that
it was upon their onus to
respond. They were bitten,
they were dying. But God
told Moses, "Make a bronze
serpent and lift it up, and
they that gaze thereon and
believe, they shall be
saved." And Moses obeyed,
and lifted up this bronze
serpent, and they were
saved.

MONTAGE OF FACES

People at the back. A SELLER OF FANS
rivetted to George - Jenny behind her,
torn between her unattended purse and
George - People at the front - one by
one - then Peter - all concentrated on
George.

                    GEORGE (O.S.)
Ah, George, you say, we are
not like unto these
Israelites. Where is the
similarity? Well, then, let
each man, let each woman
look unto their own life and
consider. How many times has
                    (MORE)

>
                    GEORGE (O.S.)
>   (CONT'D)
> the Lord delivered me? How
> many promises did I make to
> Him of undying faithfulness
> in return for his rescue?
> What, now, is the state of
> those promises? Just now
> remembered? Were you just
> complaining about your
> present circumstances?
> Murmuring against the Lord?

GEORGE'S P.O.V.

The crowd stretches out in a huge arc
around the pulpit.

>   GEORGE (O.S.)
> Do you not know that the
> Serpent is even now among
> you? The sting of death now
> reigns in your body. The
> sting of death is sin. You
> have been bitten. What are
> you to do? Go on murmuring
> as before? Or avail yourself
> of God's remedy?
> The Lord Jesus said, "If I
> am lifted up, I will draw
> all men unto myself." Do you
> not hear? Or will you just
> pass by, grumbling? Will you
> look to Him who can save
> you? Will you look to Him
> who took the very sting of
> death unto Himself for your
> sake?

ANDREW

glares across the field.

> GEORGE (O.S.)
> We will learn who is the
> wise man and who the fool by
> your answer.

GEORGE

pauses then goes in for the finish.

> GEORGE
> Oh, for the love of God, be
> reconciled unto Him. Let go
> of your complaint and let
> Him provide for you. Mind
> you, in His way and in His
> timing. For He is the very
> Bread of Heaven sent down
> for us, to sustain us. And
> He is the very Water of Life
> to quench our spiritual
> thirst.
> Praise be to His Holy Name.

DR. CORBIN'S BOOTH

Sean regroups with Egbert back by the
mountebank's stage.

> SEAN
> What do ya think?

> EGBERT
> Child's play. Could do it
> blindfolded.

Sean spots Andrew.

                         SEAN
          Sweet Fortune! I can mix
          some pleasure with business
          today!

Egbert nods to Sean and strikes out
across the field. Sean stays and
watches Andrew.

Jenny wanders and heads towards
Andrew.

ANDREW

a disgruntled Merry Andrew turns
happy, for:

ANDREW'S P.O.V.

George steps down from his pulpit and
the crowd begins to break up.

                         JENNY (O.S.)
               Well! Is this your undying
               devotion?

He looks down to see Jenny laughing up
at him.

ANDREW AND JENNY

A foul cloud masks Andrew's face, his
eyes still on his adversary.

                         ANDREW
               Now's not the time, Jen.

                         JENNY
               Jealous of your neighbor, is
               it?

A CHEER rises from across the field
and George's voice booms:

> GEORGE
> I shall return to you.

Andrew tears the cap from his head and
throws it to the ground, stamping on
it for good measure.

Highly amused, Jenny blows him a kiss
and sashays away.

NEAR GEORGE'S PULPIT

Anxiety returns to Peter as he casts
looks about him while awaiting his
turn to speak with George. JUBAL, an
older gentleman now occupies George's
attention.

> JUBAL
> Lord bless ye, sir. I'll
> have ye know that just
> awhile ago, I'd sooner break
> your head open than...But
> here you've gone and broken
> my heart.

> PETER
> If you please, sir. Can we
> talk alone?

> GEORGE
> Peter!
> (shakes Jubal's hand and
> turns to Peter)
> So good to see you!
> (he notices his

                    jitteriness)
            What's the matter, lad?

They draw apart by themselves.

                    PETER
            Mr. Whitefield, I've come to
            warn you that you are in
            danger.

                    GEORGE
            What danger is that, my boy?

                    PETER
            Someone is going to try to
            kill you.

                    GEORGE
            What? Who?

                    PETER
            I don't know his name, but I
            think I know what he looks
            like.

George motions for Peter to accompany
him to his coach. Jubal wanting to
talk further, tags along.

Egbert shadows the group.

GEORGE AND PETER

arrive at the coach, but before they
can climb into it, Egbert whips out
his sword and moves on George.

                    PETER
            Look out!

Too late. The sword already in motion
descends on George's head. Jubal steps

in and parries it with his walking
stick.

Even so the blade knocks George's wig
off. George, off-balance, hits the
ground.

Jubal tackles Egbert, and both fall in
a heap. PEOPLE from George's recent
audience pile on also, pummeling
Egbert with blows.

> GEORGE
> (Picking his wig up)
> I am all right. Please
> forbear!

Jubal and the others drag Egbert to
his feet.

> PETER
> That's him! He's the one I
> told you about!

Disarming Egbert, his captors rush him
from the field.

INT. GEORGE'S COACH

A disheveled George, sits on the bench
next to Peter, trying to still his
quaking. Hezekiah sticks his head in
the door.

> HEZEKIAH
> The pulpit's loaded and
> ready to go.

> GEORGE
> Who ordered that?

                    HEZEKIAH
          Why, it was John.

                     GEORGE
          Get him for me. And put the
          pulpit back up.

Hezekiah pops back out as fast as he
popped in.

                     PETER
          Are you all right, sir?

                     GEORGE
          I'll be fine. (Pause)
          Thanks, lad.

                     PETER
          Did you talk to Roger?
          Before--

                     GEORGE
          I have to confess that I was
          not able to--

Peter jumps to his feet.

                  GEORGE (CONT'D)
          But I did send someone in my
          place.

                     PETER
          Then you don't know if
          he's--

Peter exits the coach in a blind run,
with George calling after him.

EXT. AMONG THE VENDORS

A VENDRESS accosts the fleeing Peter.

                    VENDRESS
          Ho, there, young sir. What
          be the hurry?

She presses a pencil and some paper
into his hands. When he looks up from
his surprise, she has vanished.

PUNCH AND JUDY SHOW - LATER

Peter has found a comfortable rock by
the puppet stage. Jenny joins him.

                    JENNY
          Have you seen Tiny?

His shoulders shrug.

                    JENNY (CONT'D)
          If you do, tell him we need
          to talk.

She departs.

JENNY

strolls boldly up to the booth where
the seller of fans works. She taps the
young woman on the shoulder.

                    JENNY
          Pardon, mum. I believe you
          lost this.

Jenny takes her hand, places a small
purse in her palm and closes her
fingers around it. And walks away.

ANDREW AND JERRY

With long faces, idle in front of the
stage. The booth curtain flies open
and Dr. Corbin rushes out, giving
orders to Nicky. He strides up to
Andrew and Jerry.

>   DR. CORBIN
> And just what do you two
> think you are doing? I'm not
> paying you for polishing
> your backsides. Get to work!

>   ANDREW
> Pay? Pay? We've seen nary a
> farthing.

>   JERRY
> Hear! Hear!

>   DR. CORBIN
> There'll be no pay 'til we
> have some patrons. Now drum
> them up!

They immediately jump into action. In
their haste they almost collide with a
RECRUITING SERGEANT and a DRUMMER BOY.
Jerry screeches to a halt and Andrew
slams into him. Both about face and
beat a retreat in the other direction.
Dr. Corbin takes note of their
reaction.

LATER

Andrew and Jerry sweep the grounds
looking for patrons. They already have
Toomey in tow plus a couple others.
Andrew looks across at George and his

people.

>   TOOMEY
>   Lookee that! A prayer
>   meeting.

>   ANDREW
>   Pious philistines!

The others move on, but Andrew lags
behind. Across the field he sees Jenny
join the band of prayers. He turns
from the scene, the lines of his face
hardened.

DR. CORBIN'S BOOTH

In back, Dr. Corbin confers with
Nicky.

>   DR. CORBIN
>   I want you to find out what
>   that oaf, Jerry, has to fear
>   from lobsterbacks.

>   NICKY
>   I think I know, sir. I
>   shouldn't wonder we have a
>   deserter from His Majesty's
>   army.

>   DR. CORBIN
>   The poor dear boy. What a
>   windfall for poor dear us.

LATER

A fight breaks out in front of Dr
Corbin's stage. The combatants are
Jerry and Toomey. As they tussle back

and forth, people scoot out of the
way, not always successfully.

INT. DR. CORBIN'S BOOTH

Andrew closes the flap to the booth.

> ANDREW
> Jerry's got 'em all warmed
> up.

> DR. CORBIN
> Remember, talk up my
> abilities. We must make up
> our losses.

> ANDREW
> I'll have 'em begging for
> bottles.

EXT. DR. CORBIN'S BOOTH

Andrew slips out the back of the booth
and comes around to the front of the
stage area. He catches Jerry's eye,
then wades into the thick of the
crowd.

Jerry has Toomey in a headlock,
holding his ham of a hand
threateningly before his face. Andrew
careens into Jerry, who drops his
victim. Jerry bellows, grabs Andrew by
the shoulder and lets fly with a
haymaker. Andrew, appearing to be
struck, falls backward, but turns it
into a run of back-flips all the way
to the stage. With the last flip he
vaults onto the stage and falls into a
heap.

Andrew, satisfied all eyes are upon him, rises.

> ANDREW
> Master! Master! I am killed!
> I am killed!

He limps in a circle around the stage. In a crooked posture he stops mid-stage.

> ANDREW (CONT'D)
> Master! Master!

The crowd bubbles with CHUCKLING and appreciative CHORTLING. Dr. Corbin makes a dignified entry from behind the curtain.

> DR. CORBIN
> What now, fool?

Andrew lopes over to him.

> ANDREW
> If it please you, Master...

He holds up a limp arm with his other.

> DR. CORBIN
> Hmph. Let me see it.

Acting suspicious, he shields it from his reach.

> ANDREW
> You won't hurt me now, will you? Can't I have some of your elixir?

                    DR. CORBIN
          I shall be the judge of
          that. Lie down.

Andrew complies.

                    DR. CORBIN
                    (CONT'D)
          Now, give to me your hand.

As he stretches it towards him, the
mountebank grabs it, quickly places
his foot under Andrew's armpit and
pretends an upward jerk. Andrew jumps
up SCREAMING in mock agony, and runs
around the stage like a one-man
madhouse. And as suddenly as he began
he stops stock still, shakes the limb
and then runs joyfully around the
stage.

                    ANDREW
          I'm cured! I'm cured!

Andrew continues his celebration by
cart-wheeling up and down the stage.

PUNCH AND JUDY STAGE

Codger interrupts Peter's attention by
bounding up to him and lavishly
licking his face. Alice, in pursuit of
her dog, stumbles into his presence.

                    ALICE
          Peter?

He swings around on the rock, turning
his back to her. Something falls from
his pocket.

                    ALICE (CONT'D)
          What's the matter?

                    PETER
               (Fiercely)
          Nothing. (A beat).
          Everything!

                    ALICE
          Do you want to talk about
          it?

                    PETER
          What good would that do?
          Twouldn't change a thing...

Alice stoops to pick up what fell from
Peter's pocket.

                    PETER (CONT'D)
          ...if God couldn't change
          it, what makes you think you
          could?

She unfolds the piece of paper. It's
his sketch of her. He turns to look at
her and notices the paper. He snatches
it from her hand.

                    ALICE
          There's nothing that God
          can't do. And the sooner you
          learn that the better. And
          for whatever He doesn't do,
          there's a good reason.

The trumpet-like voice of George
Whitefield rings out from the other
side of the field.

                    GEORGE (O.S.)
          Foolish, foolish people!
               (MORE)

                              GEORGE (O.S.)
                              (CONT'D)
          Know ye not that friendship
          with the world is enmity
          towards God? And that such
          friendship that you run
          after, will ultimately
          disappoint you? Nay, it will
          ultimately destroy you. For
          such a friend is no friend
          at all, but indeed the most
          perfidious of enemies. For
          mark, he enlists your own
          will and desire to destroy
          you.

Alice jumps to her feet and grabs
Peter's hand to pull him to his feet
too.

                         ALICE
              Let's go closer.

Peter, despite his reluctance, follows
after, his hand in hers. They wend
their way through the tangle of
humanity streaming to George.

They come to rest at a spot near
Phillip-in-the-Tub.

GEORGE'S P.O.V.

The crowd gathers, for the most part
civil and meek, but at the back he
detects a ring of suspicious
characters.

                         GEORGE
              My dear brethren, I find my
                         (MORE)

                         GEORGE (CONT'D)
          heart burns within me. Set
          ablaze by a holy desire...

ANDREW AND JERRY

In front of the stage, watch as their
customers throng toward George.

                         ANDREW
          Jerry, gather everyone.
          We're going to put together
          a choir.

                         GEORGE (O.S.)
          ...a desire that will not be
          satisfied with anything less
          than each one of you coming
          into the Kingdom of God this
          very day.

BACK TO GEORGE

                         VOICE IN CROWD
          How is that, Mr. Whitefield?

                         GEORGE
          How? How indeed. It is
          really the most simple
          thing. All you need do is
          ask.

                         ANOTHER VOICE
          Why don't you stay in the
          church where you belong?

                    GEORGE
Why? That I might have the
pleasure of your company.
          (A few titter)
For, unless I'm mistaken, I
didn't see you there this
morning.
          (Loud laughter breaks
            out)
Truly, my beloved, my Master
sends me into the roads and
byways that the Gospel may
be preached.

A low rumble rises from the other side
of the field. The SHOUTS of Andrew's
mob rises in volume as well as pitch.
They drown George out and force him to
stop. George collects himself and
begins to lead in singing a hymn.
Phillip takes it up, and Alice joins
in, too. Even Peter mouths the words.

ANDREW

Agitated, turns to Jerry.

                    ANDREW
There won't be any business
until we can silence that
Bible Bigot.

                    JERRY
But, Andrew, we can't fight
against God, can we?

                    ANDREW
That man...
     (pointing across the
     field)
...is not God! He's subject
to the same laws of nature
as the rest of us.
     (he stoops and picks up
     a stone)
Go and find some more of
these.

PETER

Takes out his drawing things and
begins to sketch George.

                    GEORGE
Can we fight against God?
Ah, no, some of you are
thinking we would not even
think of such a thing. You
insist no such charge can be
laid to your door. Is that
so?

Excitement builds in Peter as the
inspiration flows out of him and onto
the paper.

                    GEORGE (CONT'D)
Perhaps a better question
would be - can we fight God
and win? For that is the
true question you are posing
in your minds and are
gambling you can.

SEAN

Notices Andrew's mob and guesses their
intent. He looks around, finds a stone
and picks it up.

> GEORGE (O.S.)
> Oh, no, you cry out. We have
> not taken arms up against
> our Creator. Right, as far
> as that goes. But let me
> point out your tactic of
> telling Him "no." And that
> to His Face. "No, I'm going
> to do it my way," is your
> refrain. However you may
> care to dress it up, or
> claim that you'll get around
> to it someday. Someday never
> comes. Today is the Day of
> the Lord. Today, if you hear
> my voice, turn from going
> your way and take up the
> path that leads to eternal
> life.

GEORGE

A hail of missiles fly over the heads
of the crowd and rain down on George.
Stones CLATTER on the ground around
him. Clods of dirt hit the pulpit and
spatter, a dead cat's head bounces off
his greatcoat and falls to his feet.

One stone out of the multitude finds
its mark, catching George on his
cheek, slicing the skin before
glancing off. George takes out a
handkerchief and calmly pats the wound
to staunch the blood.

Jenny, and Alice move closer, straining to see if George is all right.

Peter, worried, goes to look for the assailants.

George folds his handkerchief and replaces it in his pocket.

> GEORGE
> He who has an ear, let him hear. The Lord Jesus when He walked the earth came preaching, "Repent for the Kingdom of God is at hand." He told a parable about a woman, who, missing a coin, scoured her entire house 'til she found it. Who, in the same situation, would not do the same? And who, made aware of the Lord's offer, would pass by so great a treasure? Or do you esteem eternal life as but a trifle, not worth the effort of examination. Indeed, here is a treasure.
> A treasure well worth forsaking all else to be in possession of.

IN THE CROWD

Peter threads his way through the now still and silent crowd.

George begins again, but a ROARING commences from Andrew and his forces, overwhelming his voice.

The clear TENOR VOICE of Phillip-in-the-Tub soars above the roaring in the words of a hymn.

George takes up the tune and it spreads throughout the crowd. At first, the hymn seizes the high ground, but then spurred on to compete, Andrew's mob redoubles their bellowing. A seesaw battle ensues.

The hymn swells to its chorus finally drowning out Andrew.

PETER'S P.O.V.

A thwarted Andrew grabs Jerry by his elbow, and motions him to follow. Leaving the main troops to continue bellowing, Andrew guides Jerry behind their stage to the cart.

PETER

pursues them.

DR. CORBIN'S BOOTH

From the driver's seat of the wagon Andrew removes the whip.

> ANDREW
> Now, let's show 'em. Let's horsewhip us a methodist.

He turns to find Peter, blocking his path.

PETER
Don't do that, Andrew! It's
evil!

ANDREW
You! You call me evil! The
one who rescued you from
that hellhole.

PETER
You are so evil, if you're
planning to hurt Mr.
Whitefield.

ANDREW
(placating)
Don't worry, Peter. I'm only
gonna throw a scare into
him.
(takes off with Jerry in
tow)
Scare the hell into him,
that's all.

PETER

runs after them, but screeches to a
halt when Mr. Black emerges into his
path. He doesn't see Peter, because he
is intent on following Liza who has
just joined Jenny. Peter ducks into
the crowd in the opposite direction.

BEHIND GEORGE'S PULPIT

Abram joins the group of George's
supporters and takes up the hymn they
are singing. They come to the end of
the song and look up to George. There
is silence for a beat, then the

ROARING breaks out anew.

> ABRAM
> Brother George! Let us sing
> another.

George turns to his friend and nods,
then turns back to the crowd and
begins another hymn. Abram joins hands
with his friends to pray.

ANDREW

charges into the scene, sitting atop
the broad shoulders of his friend
Jerry, and waving the horsewhip above
his head. Jerry halts when he sees the
band of praying men. But Andrew digs
his heels into his ribs to urge him
on.

Abram and company step forward, to
block their progress. Andrew SNAPS the
whip at George, but misses.

GEORGE

at the CRACK of the whip, turns to see
what has happened. Andrew draws the
whip back for another attempt. George
CHUCKLES as this motion throws Andrew
off balance and tumbles him from his
perch. George turns back to the crowd
and rejoins the singing.

ANDREW

jumps back to his feet and clambers
back up onto his friend's shoulders.
And again spurs his "steed" on.

Andrew cocks the whip again, and lets
fly at George. Again his blow falls
short. Abram and his troops press
back, pushing them away from the
pulpit. Some in the crowd, now
alarmed, come around to help. Andrew
again cocks his arm, and again tumbles
to the ground.

Jerry sees the threatening crowd,
grabs the furious Andrew and retreats
from the area.

The hymn climaxes with a celebratory
chorus.

> GEORGE
> Our God is an awesome God.
> He is the Captain of a
> numberless host, and in Him
> and Him alone, we have our
> great victory.

DR. CORBIN

At the side of his stage, talks with
the recruiting sergeant.

C.U. A GOLD SOVEREIGN

Glitters in the upturned palm of the
sergeant.

> DR. CORBIN
> Do a good job, and I'll have
> a special bonus for you.

> RECRUITING
> SERGEANT
> Right you are, sir! With pleasure. Me 'n my platoon'll enfilade 'em with drumfire.

The recruiting sergeant steps to the front of his drummer, calls him to attention, and marches him out on parade.

> RECRUITING
> SERGEANT (CONT'D)
> "The Duke of Marlborough." And lively mind you!

GEORGE

surveys the silent and expectant crowd, weighing what he will say next.

> GEORGE
> It is right for us to stop in the midst of our busy lives. To stop and consider...

A flurry of DRUMBEATS rolls in like a storm and comes to a crescendo beside George's pulpit.

> GEORGE (CONT'D)
> (Sotto voce)
> O. Lord, grant me wisdom.
> (To the crowd)
> Ho there! Make way for His Majesty's officer! Clear a path!

Beginning at the front the crowd

parts, making a path that runs clear to the back. George looks down to the sergeant, and courteously indicates to him the open path.

Caught off guard the sergeant can do little else but accept the honor and marches his "platoon" through the center of the crowd.

JENNY

takes up the tune "God Save the King" and...

THE CROWD

joins in. And as the soldiers pass by, the crowd flows back together. They CHEER as the song ends.

GEORGE

holds up his hands to the crowd and rallies their attention.

>   GEORGE
>   The Lord Jesus said, "I am
>   the way, the truth and the
>   life, no man comes to the
>   Father except through me."
>   I, George Whitefield am not
>   the way. I am only like John
>   the Baptist, here to point
>   out the way to you. And that
>   way is straight and that way
>   is narrow, and few there be
>   that find it. Not because
>   they have not heard, for
>   (MORE)

> GEORGE (CONT'D)
> bless us, we live in a
> Christian nation, and the
> Lord's invitation is
> proclaimed.
> No, people do not take the
> path, because they choose
> not to. And I cannot make
> that decision for you, that
> is solely in your power.
> John the Baptist came
> calling out the children of
> Israel unto repentance.
> "Repent for the Kingdom of
> God is at hand." And I join
> with him now, in love for
> you, my countrymen, and call
> you to repentance. I place
> the choice before you today.
> Choose whom you shall serve.
> You have the prince of this
> world behind you to destroy
> you and the sea before you
> that has miraculously parted
> for your rescue.

A few TITTERS sprinkle throughout the crowd, and at the roaring faction's HOWL of delight, George faces about to discover the source of the commotion.

ANDREW

stands on the lower limb of a tree, in full view of everyone, his trousers down around his ankles.

JENNY

averts her eyes. The crowd GASPS.

C.U. STREAM OF URINE

collects in a puddle at the front of
the tree. Andrew's mob now ROARS with
hilarity.

GEORGE

seizes the railing in front and wrests
back the attention of the crowd.

> GEORGE
> Is there any among you now
> who would dispute the saying
> that man, when left to
> himself, is half a devil and
> half a beast needing wholly
> to be reborn?

Andrew's mob is struck silent. One by
one their numbers dwindle, with most
joining the quiet, listening crowd.

> GEORGE (O.S.)
> (CONT'D)
> Aye, you know it to be true.
> You look around at one
> another and see it. You mark
> well whereat your brother
> has offended you. But you
> fail to put yourself under
> examination, you see not
> where you yourself come
> short. We lavish all the
> excuses on ourselves, and
> mete out all the blame to
> others.

LIZA

watches riveted.

>   GEORGE (O.S.)
>   All have sinned and fall
>   short of the glory of God.
>   Not a one of us has a reason
>   to boast to the contrary.
>   Not a one of us is righteous
>   enough to stand in the
>   presence of a Holy God.

In Liza comprehension dawns.

ANDREW

clenches his jaw, and stamps over to
Jerry and Toomey. He says not a word.
He is too enraged. He looks across to
the empty maypole. A wolfish grin
crosses his lips.

>   ANDREW
>   I'm not finished yet!

He attacks the pole as if he could
drag it out by himself. Jerry moves
alongside, and soon wrenches it from
the earth. Nicky joins the trio as
they heave up the make-shift battering
ram.

PETER

hiding from Black, peers out to look
around.

PETER'S P.O.V.

Andrew's juggernaut charges straight
towards George and his pulpit.

In their path lie Jenny, Liza, Alice and Codger. And Tiny, all unsuspecting.

> PETER (O.S.)
> Andrew! Jerry! No!
> (prays)
> Heavenly Father, help us!

TINY

turns and sees the imminent danger. And Sean who is bearing down on Andrew, ready to strike.

SEAN

whips his knife out and launches himself at Andrew.

SEAN'S P.O.V.

A wall of fire appears between him and Andrew. A wall no one else can see.

TINY'S P.O.V.

Unaccountably Sean plummets to the ground.

GEORGE'S P.O.V.

The crowd at the back parts before the men carrying the pole. All of a sudden their forward advance stops dead, the front of the pole dips to the ground, and Andrew still clinging to the back end of the pole rises above the heads of the crowd, then crashes to the ground out of George's sight.

JERRY

stands over the struggling body of Nicky.

> JERRY
> Betray me, will you?

Jerry makes to plant his boot on the man's face, but Nicky catches it in his hands and twists it, forcing Jerry off balance. As Jerry topples, however, he falls full force back on Nicky.

ANDREW

lies in a mudhole, his butt sticking up in the air and the maypole resting on his head, buried in the mud.

TINY

kneels by Sean, and comes away with his knife.

GEORGE'S P.O.V.

The crowd at the back attacks the former assailants, who flee helter-skelter.

> GEORGE (O.S.)
> Forbear! Return not evil for evil.

LIZA

the tears fresh on her cheeks, hugs
her sister Jenny. Over her sister's
shoulder she spots Peter.

                    LIZA
          Peter!

As Peter takes his first halting steps
towards his mother, Mr. Black runs up
to intercept him.

PETER

freezes in terror. But a gust of wind
blows up, rips his drawing from his
grip and plasters it over Black's
head, blinding him. Peter flees back
into the densely packed crowd
surrounding George.

                    GEORGE
          Let us not join the side of
          the Enemy for any reason.
          Nor plunge ourselves into
          hell at his whim. Let us
          rather give God our whole
          hearts, and no longer halt
          between two opinions.

TINY

vacillates, shifting from one leg to
the other. Then casts the die and
steps forward, joining those who are
listening to George.

                    GEORGE
You cannot serve two
masters. Christ came down to
purchase our hearts. Should
we give Him only half? Alas,
why should we be so in love
with slavery that we will
not wholly renounce the
world, the flesh and the
devil which, like so many
spiritual chains, bind down
our souls and hinder them
from flying up to God. The
Father of your souls awaits.
The Lord Jesus awaits. Come!
I say, come, to the lover of
your souls.

ANDREW

defeated, turns his back and leaves.

IN FRONT OF GEORGE'S PULPIT

Abram helps George collect notes from
the people wanting prayer. He spots
Peter.

                    ABRAM
          Ho, there! Peter!

Abram walks up to him.

                    ABRAM (CONT'D)
          Am I glad to see you! I've a
          message for you from Mr.
          Morgan.

Abram puts an arm around his shoulder
and walks him back towards George.

ABRAM (CONT'D)
He wants you to know that
he'll be seeing you again.
And to that end he wanted me
to be sure you understood
that he became a Christian
before he died.

Peter hugs a surprised Abram and then
dashes to George.

GEORGE
You know, Peter, Roger is in
Heaven as we speak.

PETER
I know! I know!

Mr. Black blusters into their midst.

BLACK
I'll thank ye to hand over
my 'prentice.

Abram steps between them.

ABRAM
I'm going to ask you to
prove your master's status,
sir.

Mr. Black stabs out a bony finger at
Peter.

BLACK
He's mine, I tell ya!

GEORGE
That, sir, we shall refer to
the parish authorities to
decide.

                    BLACK
          I demand my rights...

He lunges to catch Peter by his arm,
but Abram, intercepts him and forces
his arm behind his back and locks it
there.

                    ABRAM
          You will leave this area at
          once. Don't worry about your
          "property,"he is in good
          hands. And you shall see him
          again before the magistrate
          when I bring in an order for
          an enquiry into your
          stewardship of your
          apprentices.

Abram releases him. Mr. Black slinks
off.

INT. THE GLOBE AND URINAL/ANDREW AND
JERRY'S ROOM - LATER

Andrew haunts the window, looking but
not seeing. Jerry's entrance shrinks
the room.

                    JERRY
          'Lo Andrew.

                    ANDREW
          Where've you been ?

                    JERRY
          Down at Moorfields.
          Talking... You know, Andrew,
          things aren't as bad as they
          seem...

                    ANDREW
          Good God! You've become one
          of them, haven't you?

                    JERRY
          Don't blaspheme, Andrew.

                    ANDREW
          Damn. Now I see it all. I
          shoulda seen it coming. All
          day you've been sympathetic
          to them. You're the one
          responsible...

                    JERRY
          That's right, I'm the one
          who dropped the maypole.
          Everything's my fault.
          Nothin's ever yer fault,
          Andrew!

He draws out Sean's dagger and sticks
it in the bed post.

                    JERRY (CONT'D)
          There! It woulda been yours
          anyway! Tiny took it off of
          the man who was goin' to
          stick it into you.

Andrew staggers.

Jerry clumps to the door.

                    JERRY (CONT'D)
          It wasn't luck that saved
          you. One way or other
          nothing was gonna stop that
          meeting.

He slams the door.

EXT. ABRAM'S HOUSE - DAY

Abram puts his arm around Peter and they start out down the street.

> ABRAM
> Well, lad, what would you say to becoming my apprentice in the sign-painting trade?

Peter leaps with joy into his arms.

> ABRAM (CONT'D)
> And I think I can use your friend Jerry.

> PETER
> Oh, yes! Yes!

From the end of the street Alice and Codger run to meet them.

EXT MOORFIELDS - DAY

The field bears the scars of yesterday, trampled grass and churned earth and debris strewn throughout. The early morning breeze plays with the debris, blowing it here and there. One large piece of paper blows flat against a rock wall.

PETER'S SKETCH

George preaches from his pulpit. Above him are chariots of fire and angels dressed for battle.

                    GEORGE (V.O.)
          You know, Peter, Roger is in
          Heaven as we speak.

And around the chariots and angels
flocks a great crowd of witnesses, but
all we can make out is the features of
one - Roger Morgan.

                    PETER (V.O.)
          I know! I know!

The wind snatches it away.

FADE OUT

THE END

AFTERWARD

The genesis for this screenplay dates back to the late 1980s. It was an era in my life when I was devouring histories and biographies about 18th Century England, and, in particular, biographies about the Evangelicals of the time. I sought out books about men like the Wesleys, (John and Charles), John Newton, Granville Sharp, and George Whitefield. My original focus was the life of William Wilberforce, the member of Parliament and Christian who led the fight to abolish the slave trade in the British Empire.

Actually I had started a script on Wilber - a musical play to be exact. (His bubbly personality in my estimation is tailor made for the form). Along the way, the person of the great Evangelist, George Whitefield captured my imagination. Many of the events of his life were exciting, and I could visualize them as a better subject for a movie than a play.

So, I added this as a second project to my plate. At first, I worked on both projects in long hand. And after I was given a cast-off word processor from my work office, I was writing them and storing the results on floppy disks. Come 1990 and the advent of the writing software program Final Draft (for whom I was a beta tester), I transferred what I had thus far into my PC and this new program.

I must have had the first two acts completed on Wilber, when I realized I was making a lot more headway on the George Whitefield project than the musical. Originally George was the central figure of this screenplay which I had entitled 'White Unto Harvest,' a reference to the time when Jesus was praying that more laborers be sent out into the fields to bring in the harvest. (Here, it was referring to spiritual matters, people were out there and ready to be gathered into the Kingdom of God). But I decided to move George out of the spotlight to more of a supporting role. And I created a character, young Peter Micklewhite, a fatherless chimney sweep, around whom to build the story.

In the midst of writing the now titled 'Peter and the Dragon,' I heard about, and enrolled in a screenwriting class at the Film Studies Center in Portland Oregon in 1993. My fellow students and the instructor Roger Margolis were helpful and encouraging. And Roger was quite complimentary when I supplied him with a copy of my completed script in 1996.

But where to take it next?

My day job at that time was as an accountant for the Act III Theater circuit, headquartered in Portland, Oregon. In that capacity I had lots of contacts with the film studios in LA - exclusively in the distribution end of the business, however - and not with producers.

Sometime that same year, I read in an article that a Christian thriller novel "This Present Darkness," was now in the process of being brought to the screen in Hollywood. This news excited me greatly for I had read the book and liked it very much. I asked one of my contacts, Tim Penland, who had distributed a Christian film (China Cry) in 1990, if he knew anything about the producer. He had, and told me that the producer, Howard Kazanjian was a believer. He also supplied me with some contact information.

I wrote Howard just to ask him about his new project. He very graciously answered my letter and thanked me for my interest. In a follow-up letter I told him that I was looking for representation as a writer and asked him if he knew of any agents that were Christian. Again he very kindly pointed me to a Christian organization that has a ministry to those in the film industry. Through this ministry, Master Media International, I received three possibilities to contact.

A year later, after two of the individuals had replied in the negative, I was still waiting for word back from the third. I again wrote Howard to ask what that might mean - he replied that a no answer was usually a 'no.' I screwed up the courage to ask if he might read my screenplay (now entitled Peter and the Serpent).

After I signed a release, Howard agreed to do so. A month later, he wrote back to me - he liked the script and complimented me on "a wonderful job in the writing." But it was not a story that he thought he could set up, and passed on it. He did kindly offer to send it on to two film financiers.

Historical (or period) scripts are notoriously hard to set up, and at that time even more so for a faith based one. I was not discouraged when the answers, one by one, came back in the negative. I was content with what I had written. And I was then on to my next project.

COMING SOON

I am excited to announce that I will be publishing my second film script in March of 2023.

It is entitled Running Out of Sky.

A brash young Army pilot elopes with his childhood sweetheart over the objection of her father, only to be separated the next day by the outbreak of WW2. With mounting misunderstandings and her father's active efforts to sabotage their relationship, motivated by a past family betrayal, they each struggle to remain true to their vows - she on the home-front and he in the forbidden skies over China.

Also, my second collection of poetry called Body Life in the First Tuesday Poetry series will appear in June of 2023.

Look for the Barnabas Press page on Facebook.

Or my website: barnabaspress.net

ABOUT THE PUBLISHER

Barnabas Press

I created the Barnabas Press, registering it as a business in the State of Washington in May of 2022. It has always been my intent to select this title as a production entity. This springs from the time long ago when we were studying in the Book of Acts in the New Testament at church. During that study I learned about the man called Barnabas, who was a mentor and friend to the Pharisee Saul (who became the Apostle Paul). This individual was a Jewish Levite by the name of Joseph from the island of Cyprus. After his personal sacrifices to help the young church in Jerusalem, the apostles there gave him the special name of Barnabas - which has as its meaning - "the son of encouragement."

This defines the purpose behind my press. I am hoping to encourage my readers through the publication of my writings.

RWOz2

ABOUT THE AUTHOR

I am a poet, an historian, a novelist, and a writer for stage and screen, but foremost a responder to Jesus (Romans 5:8).

I was employed for over forty years in the entertainment industry, the last thirty of which I have crunched numbers successively for three of the top ten theater circuits in the US.

Back then my forte was numbers, added up in columns and balanced. Now I am hard at work exploring the richness of existence in a passion for words. Words that add up into poems, works of fiction and non, and works to be performed.

I am currently writing my fourth novel, looking out from my window onto the great Pacific Northwest, where I live with my wife Karen.

Join me as I follow the Word

Lightning Source UK Ltd.
Milton Keynes UK
UKHW041045211222
414263UK00001B/89

9 798201 353360